Anna Vivanti

The Outrage

Outlook

Anna Vivanti

The Outrage

1. Auflage | ISBN: 978-3-73262-466-9

Erscheinungsort: Frankfurt am Main, Deutschland

Erscheinungsjahr: 2018

Outlook Verlag GmbH, Frankfurt.

THE OUTRAGE

ANNIE VIVANTI CHARTRES

NEW YORK : ALFRED A. KNOPF : 1918

THE OUTRAGE

BOOK I

CHAPTER I

Chérie was ready first. She flung her striped bath-robe over her shoulders and picked up Amour who was wriggling and barking at her pink heels.

"*Au revoir dans l'eau,*" she said to little Mireille and to the German nursery governess, Frieda.

"Oh, Frieda, *vite, vite, dégrafez-moi,*" cried Mireille, backing towards the hard-faced young woman and indicating a jumble of knotted tapes hanging down behind her.

"Speak English, please, both. This is our English day," said Frieda, standing in her petticoat-bodice in front of the mirror and removing what the girls called her "Wurst" from the top of her head. In the glass she caught sight of Chérie making for the door and called her back sharply. "Mademoiselle Chérie, you go not in the street without your stockings and your hat."

"Nonsense, Frieda! In Westende every one goes to bathe like this," and Chérie waved a bare shapely limb and flicked her pink toes at Amour, who barked wildly at them.

"I do not care how every one goes. You go not," said Frieda Rothenstein, hanging her sleek brown Wurst carefully on the mirror-stand.

"Then what have we come here for?" sulked Chérie, dropping Amour and giving him a soft kick with her bare foot.

"We have come here," quoth Frieda, "not for marching our undressed legs about the streets, but for the enjoyment both of the summer-freshness and of the out-view." Whereupon Mireille gave a sudden shriek of laughter and Amour bounded round her and barked.

Chérie crossed the room to the chair on which her walking clothes had been hastily flung. "Won't sand-shoes do?"

"No. Sand-shoes and stockings," said Frieda. "And hat," she added, glancing down at the comely bent head with its cascade of waving red-brown locks.

Chérie hurriedly drew on her black stockings, glancing up occasionally to smile at Mireille; and nothing could be sweeter than those shining eyes seen through the veil of falling hair. Now she was ready, her flapping *bergère* hat crushed down on her careless curls, Amour hoisted under her arm again, and with a nod of commiseration to Mireille she ran down the narrow wooden staircase of Villa Esther, Madame Guillaume's *appartements meublés* and was down in the rue des Moulins with her smiling face to the sea.

The street was a short one, half of it not yet built over, leading from a new aeroplane-shed at the back to the wide asphalted promenade on the sea-front. Chérie met some other bathers—a couple of men striding along in their bathing suits, their bronzed limbs bare, a damp towel round their necks, their wet hair plastered to their cheeks. They barely glanced at the picturesque little figure in the brief red bathing-skirt and flapping hat, for all along the sands— from Nieuport, twenty minutes to the right, to Ostend half an hour to the left —there were hundreds of just such charming school-girl figures darting about in the sunlight, while all the fast and loose "daughters of joy" from Brussels, Namur, and Spa, added their more poignant note of provocativeness to the blue and gold beauty of the summer scene.

Chérie passed the bicycle shop and waved a friendly hand to Cyrille Wibon, who was kneeling before his racing Petrolette and washing its shining nose with the tenderness of a nurse and the pride of a father.

"Remember! the two bicycles at eleven, on the sands," cried Chérie in Flemish, and Cyrille lifted a quick forefinger to his black hair, and nodded. Chérie ran on, crossed the wide promenade, and skipped down the shallow flight of steps leading to the sands, those vast sweeping sands of Westende that begin and end in the wide, wild dunes. She dropped Amour, who rolled over, righted himself, dug a few rapid holes with his hind paws in the sand and then trotted off to lead his own wicked dog's life with certain hated enemies of his—a supercilious leveret, a scatter-brained Irish terrier, and a certain mean and shivering black-and-tan, whose tastes and history would not bear investigation.

Chérie plunged through the quarter of a mile of dry, soft sand, into which her feet sank at every step, and as she reached the smoother surface that the outgoing tide left hard and level, she flung off her bath-robe and her hat, her sand-shoes and her stockings; then she ran out into the water.

Lithe and light she ran, skipping over the first shallow waves and on until the water lapped her knees and the red skirt bulged out all round her like a balloon—on she ran with little chilly gasps of delight, raising her white arms above her head as the water rose and encircled her with its cool, strong embrace. The sun cast a net of dancing diamonds on the blue satin sea, and the girl felt the joy of life bound within her like some wild, living thing. She joined her finger-tips and dived into the dancing waters; then she emerged, pushing her wet hair from her eyes with her wet hand. She swam on and on toward the azure horizon, and dreamed of thus swimming on for ever and losing herself in the blue beauty of the world.

An aeroplane passed above her with its angry whirr returning from Blankenberghe to Nieuport, and she turned on her back and floated, looking up at it and waving her small gleaming hand. She thought the plane dipped suddenly as if it would fall upon her, and she watched it, holding her breath for the pilot's safety till it was almost out of sight. Then she turned and trod water awhile and blinked at the distant shore for a sight of Mireille.

Yes, surely, there was the skimpy figure of Frieda, and beside it ran and hopped the still skimpier figure of Mireille, whose thin legs had only scampered through ten Aprils and whose treble voice cut the distance with the shrill note of exceeding youth.

"Chéreee!… Chéreeee!… Come back. Come back and fetch me!"

So Chérie, with a sigh, turned and swam slowly landward.

Mireille came running out to meet her with little splashes and jumps and shrieks, while Frieda stopped behind in a few inches of water and went through a series of hygienic rites, first wetting her forehead, then her chest, then her forehead again, and finally sitting down solemnly in the water until she had counted a hundred. This concluded her bath, and she went home to dress.

When, an hour later, she came down to the sands again neatly clothed in her Reformkleid, with the Wurst reinstated high and dry on the top of her otherwise damp head, she saw her two charges lying flat and motionless in the sand, the broiling sunshine burning down on their upturned faces and closed eyes. They were pretending to be dead; and indeed, thought Frieda, as she saw them lying, so small and still on the immensity of the sands, they looked like drowned morsels of humanity tossed up by the sea.

Before Frieda could reach them, Cyrille, the bicycle teacher, passed her—the monkey-man, as the girls called him—pedalling along on one machine and guiding the other towards the two small recumbent figures. They jumped up when they heard him, and by the time Frieda reached the spot, Mireille was being hoisted on to a very rusty old machine, while Chérie, a slim, scarlet figure, with auburn locks afloat and white limbs gleaming, was skimming along in the distance on the smooth resilient sands.

"I do not approve," panted Frieda, running alongside of the swaying Mireille, while the monkey-man trotted behind and held the saddle,—"I do not approve of this bicycle-riding in bathing costume."

"Oh, Frieda," gasped Mireille, "do stop scolding, you make me wobble—" and with a sudden swerve the bicycle described a semicircle and ran swiftly down into the sea.

Mireille was very angry with Frieda and with the bicycle and with the monkey-man, who grinned with his very white teeth in his very dark face, and hoisted her up again. Frieda soon tired of following them, and sat down near an empty boat to read *Der Trompeter von Säkkingen.*

Säkkingen! As Frieda's eyes skimmed the neatly printed pages and lingered on the woodcut of a church tower and a bridge, her soul went back to the little town on the Rhine. For Frieda, like the famous trumpeter, came from Säkkingen; her feet, in square German shoes, had tottered and run and clattered and tripped at divers ages over its famous covered bridge; she had leaned out of the small flower-filled windows, and sent her girlish dreams floating down the sleepy waters of the Rhine; she had passed Victor von Sheffel's small squat monument every morning on her way to school, and every evening on her way home she had looked up at the shuttered windows of the house that had been his. Säkkingen!—with its clean white streets and its blue-and-white Kaffee-Halle in the Square and its bakeries redolent of fresh *Kuchen* and *Schnecken*.... Frieda raised eyes of rancour to the dancing North Sea, to the smooth Belgian sands, to the distant silhouettes of Chérie, Mireille, and the monkey-man, even to the bounding Amour and his companions of iniquity. She hated it all. She hated them all. They were all selfish and vulgar and flippant, with no poetry in their souls, and no religion, and bad cooking.... Frieda shook her head bitterly: "*Das Land das meine Sprache spricht ...*" she murmured in nostalgic tones, and sighed. Then she took up her book again and read what Hidigeigei, tom-cat and philosopher, had to say about love and the Springtime.

> Warum küssen sich die Menschen?
> Warum meistens nur die Jungen?
> Warum diese meist im Frühjahr?...

That evening Mireille opened the door to the postman and took two letters from him. Then she went to the sitting-room where Frieda and Chérie sat at their needlework; hiding one of the letters behind her back she read out the superscription of the other with irritating slowness:

"Mademoiselle—Chérie—Brandès—Villa—Esther—"

"Oh, give it to me!" cried Chérie, extending an impatient hand.

"It is from Loulou," said Mireille, giving up the letter and still holding the other one behind her back.

"You may not call your mother Loulou," snapped Frieda. "I have never heard of such a thing."

"She likes it," said Mireille. "Besides, Chérie calls her Loulou."

"Chérie is her sister-in-law, not her daughter," said Frieda; then catching sight of the other letter in Mireille's hand: "Who is that for?"

"Hochwohlgeborenes Fräulein—Frieda Rothenstein—" read Mireille, and Frieda rose quickly and pulled the letter out of her hand. "Oh, Frieda, you rude thing! Who is your letter from? It's on our letter-paper, and is not from Loulou, and it is not from my father. Who calls you all that twiddly-twaddly *hochwohlgeboren* nonsense?"

Nobody answered. Both Fräulein and Chérie were reading their letters with intent eyes. Mireille continued her monologue. "I believe it is from Fritz. Fancy! Fritz, who is only papa's servant, writing to you! Do you answer him? Fancy a *hochwohlgeboren* getting letters from a man-servant!"

Frieda did not deign to reply, nor did she raise her eyes from the letter in her hand; yet as Mireille could see, it was only one line long. Just four or five words. But Frieda sat staring at them as if they had turned her to stone.

Now Chérie had finished reading the hastily scrawled page in her hand and raised a face full of consternation.

"Frieda! Mireille! Do you know what has happened? We are to go home tomorrow."

"Tomorrow!" exclaimed Mireille. "Why, papa said we were to stay here two months, and we only arrived four days ago."

"Well, your mother writes that we are to go home at once. Do you hear, Frieda?" But Frieda did not answer nor raise her eyes.

"But why—why?" cried Mireille. "Doesn't Loulou know we have arranged to have your birthday party here, with Lucile and Jeannette and Cri-cri all coming on purpose?"

"Yes, she knows," said Chérie, turning her sweet, perplexed eyes from Mireille's disconcerted face to the impassive countenance of Frieda, "but she says there is going to be war."

"War? What has that got to do with us?" exclaimed Mireille in injured tones. "It really is too bad. Just as I had made up my mind that tomorrow I would swim with both feet off the ground!..."

CHAPTER II

The next day's sun rose hot and angry. It was the 30th of July. By ten o'clock Frieda had packed everything. Amour had been put into his picnic-basket and his humped-up back coaxed and patted and finally forcibly pressed down, and the lid shut over him. Then they awaited the carriage ordered by telephone from Ostend the night before.

But no carriage arrived. At eleven Chérie ran across to the telephone-office and spoke in her sternest tones to the livery stable in Ostend.

"*Eh bien?* Is this carriage coming? We ordered it for ten o'clock."

"No, Madame, it is not coming," replied a gruff voice from the other end.

"Not coming?"

"No, Madame." Then in lower, almost confidential tones, "It has been requisitioned."

"What is that? Then send another one," said Chérie. But Ostend had cut off the communication and Chérie returned crestfallen and wondering to the glum Frieda and the doleful Mireille sitting on the trunks in Madame Guillaume's narrow hall.

"No carriage," she said.

"What?" exclaimed Frieda.

"Why not?" asked Mireille.

"I don't know; something is being done to it," Chérie said vaguely. "I did not understand. Perhaps it is being re—re—covered, or something."

At noon Madame Guillaume found a porter for them who wheeled the luggage on a hand-cart to the Westende tramway station. And the tramway carried them and their luggage and Amour in his basket to Ostend, where another man with a hand-cart was found to wheel the luggage and the basket to the railway station.

They noticed at once that Ostend wore a strange and novel air. Crowds filled the town, crowds that were not the customary sauntering demi-mondaines and lounging viveurs. No; the streets were full of hurrying people, of soldiers on foot and on horseback; long lines of motor-cars, motor-cycles, carts and wagons blocked the roadways, and behind them came peasants leading strings of unharnessed horses. Down the rue Albert came, marching rapidly, a little band of Gardes Civiques in their long coats and incongruous bowler-hats with

13

straps under their chins. Groups of officers, who had arrived a few days before for the international tennis tournament, were assembled on the Avenue Leopold and talked together in low, eager tones.

"What is the matter with everybody?" asked Mireille, as they hurried through the Place St. Joseph and across the bridge after the man with the luggage, who was already vanishing into the crowded station.

As if in answer to her question a couple of newspaper boys came rushing past with shrill cries. "*Supplément ... supplément de 'l'Indépendance' ..., Mobilization Générale....*"

"Frieda, is there really going to be war?" asked Chérie, looking anxiously at Frieda's sulky profile.

"Yes, I believe so," said Frieda. "Between Russia and Germany."

"Oh well; that is far away," said young Chérie, with a little laugh of relief, and she ran to rescue the picnic-basket from the porter's roughly swinging hand.

"Amour is whining," whispered Mireille, as they stood in the crush waiting to pass the ticket-collector on the quai.

"Oh! he mustn't," said Chérie. "Officially he is sandwiches."

So Mireille thumped the basket with her small gloved hand and murmured, "*Couche-toi, tais-toi, vilian scélérat.*" And the official sandwiches subsided in the basket and were silent.

They never had such a journey. The train was crowded to suffocation; the whole world seemed to be going to Brussels; every few minutes their train stopped to let other even more crowded trains dash past them towards the capital.

"I have never seen so many soldiers," said Mireille. "I did not think there were so many in the world."

Frieda Rothenstein smiled disdainfully with the corners of her mouth turned down. "There are a few more than this in my country," she said.

"What? In Germany? But not such beautiful ones," cried Mireille, hanging out of the window and waving her handkerchief as many others did to a little company of Lancers cantering past on the winding road with lances fixed and pennants fluttering.

Frieda glanced at them superciliously. "You should see our Uhlans," she said. And added under her breath, "Who knows? Perhaps one day you may."

But the girls were not listening. The train was running into Brussels at last.

The journey had taken five hours instead of two.

An hour later they still sat in the motionless train in the Brussels station.

"At this rate we shall never reach Bomal," said Chérie drearily, as they watched train after train packed with soldiers leave the station before theirs in the direction of Liège. Here all the world seemed to be rushing out of Brussels towards the eastern frontier.

But all things end; and finally their train started too, panting and puffing out of the Gare du Nord towards Louvain, Tirlemont, and Liège.

It was utterly dark by the time they reached Liège; and when they left the Gare Guillemin the soft summer night had swathed the valley of the Ourthe with tenebrous draperies. Little Mireille fell asleep with a pale smudgy face resting against Frieda's arm. Chérie lay back in her corner dozing and dreaming of Westende's blue sea; but Frieda's eyes were wide open staring out into the darkness as the train rumbled in and out of the tunnels, clattered over bridges following the gleaming blackness of the river.

Where the Ourthe meets its younger brother the Aisne, the train slowed down, trembled, hissed, and stopped.

"Bomal," announced the guard.

"Here we are! Mireille, wake up!" cried Chérie, looking out of the window. Then she put Mireille's *bergère* hat very crookedly on the child's towzled head, while Frieda hurriedly collected the books, the tennis-rackets and the parasols.

"Ah! there he is," and Chérie waved her hand out of the window to a tall figure on the platform. "Claude! Claude! *Nous voici.*"

Claude Brandès, a handsome man, fifteen years older than his sister Chérie, opened the carriage door with an exclamation of relief. "Thank goodness you are here," he said, lifting his dazed, weary little daughter in his arms as if she were a baby and hoisting her on to his shoulder. "Are you all right? Have you got everything? Come along!" And he started down the platform, Chérie and Frieda trotting quickly after him. "Mademoiselle," he said, turning to Frieda, "give the check for your trunks to Fritz."

"*Oui, Monsieur le Docteur,*" she replied, fumbling for it in her hand-bag. Then she looked round for the man-servant, whom she had as yet not caught sight of. Fritz Hollander ("Hollander by name and Hollander by nationality," he always said of himself when making new acquaintances) stepped out of the shadow and took the paper from Frieda's hand. She murmured a greeting to him, but he did not reply nor did he seem to notice her questioning glance. He

15

turned on his heel, and his massive figure was soon swallowed up in the shadows at the end of the station.

The little party had just reached the exit and the train, with a parting whistle, was curving away into the darkness, when Mireille suddenly raised her face from her father's shoulder and gave a shriek. "Amour! We have forgotten Amour!"

It was true. Amour, cramped and disgusted in his creaky luncheon basket, was travelling away in the darkness to the heart of the Ardennes.

After the first moment of dismay everybody was cross with everybody else.

"It's all his own fault," said Chérie, who was tired and hungry. "He might have barked. He knew perfectly well that we were getting out."

"Haven't we taught him to pretend he is sandwiches when we're travelling?" sobbed Mireille indignantly. "How can you be so unjust?"

"Never mind, Mirette," said her father; "don't cry. We will telegraph to Marché to have him stopped and sent back. You will see him turn up safe and tail-wagging in the morning."

And the telegram was sent.

As they walked through the silent, sleeping village of Bomal Chérie inquired, "Why is Loulou not here? She might have come in the motor."

Her brother hesitated a moment. "I have sent away the car," he said.

"Sent it away? What for?" exclaimed Chérie.

"I have ... I have lent it," said Dr. Brandès.

"To whom?" inquired Mireille, trotting beside her father and hanging on to his arm.

He gave a little laugh. "To the King," he said.

"Oh!" cried Mireille. "Not much of a car to lend to a king! Surely he has better ones himself."

"We all give what we have in time of war," said her father. "Come, I will carry you, my little bird," he said, and lifted her up again.

"What is the matter? Why are you so affectionate?" asked Mireille, nestling comfortably in his arms and patting his broad back with her small hand.

Chérie laughed and looked up adoringly at her big brother. "Is he not always affectionate?" she asked.

"Not so dreadfully," replied Mireille, in her matter-of-fact tones; and then they all three laughed.

Frieda, hurrying behind them in the dark with the books, the parasols, and the tennis-rackets, hated them for their laughter.

Louise Brandès, a slim white figure in the moonlight, awaited them at the door. She kissed Mireille and Chérie and greeted Frieda kindly; then she made them all drink hot milk and sent them to bed.

"But I want to tell papa about how I can almost swim and nearly ride a bicycle," said Mireille, sidling up to her father.

"You shall tell him tomorrow, my darling," said Louise.

But the morrow was not as they dreamed it.

When early next morning Frieda and the girls came down to the breakfast-room they found Louise, still in her white dress of the evening before, sitting on the sofa with red eyes and a pale face. In answer to their anxious questioning she told them that Claude had been called away. Two officers had come for him close upon midnight; he had scarcely had time to pack a few things. He had taken his surgical outfit; then they had hurried him away with short words and anxious faces.

"But where—where has he gone to?" asked Chérie.

"I don't know," said her sister-in-law, and the tears gathered in her dark eyes. "They said something about his being sent to a field ambulance, or to … to the Dépôt Central…."

"What is that?" asked Mireille; but as nobody knew, nobody answered.

Mariette the maid brought in the breakfast, followed by her mother, Marie the cook; and they both had red eyes and were weeping. Marie said that her two sons had come to the house at dawn to bid her and Mariette good-bye; the eldest, Toinot, belonged to the 9th line regiment and had been sent off to Stavelot; and Charles, the youngest, had volunteered and was being sent off heaven knows where.

"Of course there is nothing to cry about," added Marie, with large round tears rolling down her ruddy face. "There is no danger for our country. But still—to see one's boys—going away like that—s-s-singing the B-b-brabançonne—" she broke into sobs.

"Of course, my good Marie," echoed Louise, "there is nothing to cry about...."

And then they all wept bitterly. Even Frieda, with her face in her handkerchief, sobbed—on general principles, and also because Weltschmerz gnawed at her treacherous, sentimental German heart.

At breakfast every one felt a little better. As nearly all the men had left Bomal or were about to leave, it was a comfort to reflect that Fritz Hollander, the doctor's confidential servant, being a Dutchman, was not obliged to go. True, he was a somewhat sulky, taciturn person, but he had been with them two years and, as Loulou remarked while she poured out the coffee, one felt that one could trust him.

"I always trust people who are silent and look straight at you when you speak," said the wise Louise, who was twenty-eight years old, and admired Georges Ohnet.

"I don't like Fritz," remarked Mireille. "I hate the shape of his head—and especially his ears," she added.

"Don't be silly," said Chérie.

Frieda, who was just dipping a fresh roll into her coffee, looked up. "He has the ears God gave him," she remarked, with pinched and somewhat tremulous lips.

Every one looked at her wonderingly, and she flushed scarlet as she bent her head and dipped her roll into her cup again.

After breakfast Louise went to rest for a few hours; Frieda said she had some letters to write, and the two girls went out to call on their friends and make plans as to what they would do on Chérie's birthday, the 4th of August.

They went to Madame Doré's house in the Place du Marché and found their friends Cécile and Jeannette busy with their boy-scout brother, André; they were sewing a band with S.M. on it, on the right sleeve of his green shirt.

"What is S.M.?" inquired Mireille.

"That means Service Militaire," replied André proudly.

"Fancy!" exclaimed Mireille. "And you only fifteen!"

André passed his left hand carelessly over his fair hair. "Oh yes," he said, with very superior nonchalance. "There are four thousand of us. We shall have to take care of you women," he glanced with raised eyebrows at the small, admiring Mireille, "now that the other men have gone."

"Keep your arm quiet," said Cécile, "or I shall prick you."

"Where is your father?" asked Chérie. "Has he left, too?"

"Yes," said André. "He has been called out for duty in the Garde Civique. He is stationed on the Chaussée de Louvain, not far from Brussels."

"Isn't it all exciting?" cried Jeannette, jumping up and down.

"But against whom are we going to fight?" asked Mireille.

"We don't know yet," declared André. "Perhaps against the French; perhaps against the Germans."

"Perhaps against nobody," said Cécile, biting off the thread and patting the neatly-sewn armlet on her brother's sleeve.

"Perhaps against nobody," echoed André, with a boyish touch of ruefulness. "Nobody will dare to invade our land."

"Come, let us go into the garden," said Jeannette.

Thus it was in Belgium on the eve of her impending doom. Doubtless in high places—in the Palais de la Nation and the Place Royale—there were hearts filled with racking anxiety and feverish excitement; but throughout the country there was merely a sense of resolute expectancy, of not altogether unpleasant excitement. Every one knew that the sacrosanct rights of the land would be respected, but it was just as good, they said, to be ready for every event.

Nobody on that summer evening, from the remotest corner of Belgian Luxembourg to the farthest homestead in Flanders, as they watched that last July sun go down over the peaceful fields of grain, dreamed that the Grey Wolves of War were already snarling at the gates, straining to be let loose and overrun the world, panting to get to their work of slaughter and destruction. No one dreamed that four days later massacre and outrage and frenzied ferocity would rage through the shuddering valleys of the Ardennes.

Thus while Chérie and Cécile, Jeannette and Mireille ran out into their sunshiny garden, at that same hour, far away in the Wilhelmstrasse a man with a grey beard stood on a balcony and spoke to a surging crowd— promising blood to the wolves.

Thus while the four fair girls planned what they would do on the 4th of August, on that balcony in Berlin their fate and the fate of Europe was being pronounced.

"We shall invite Lucile, Cri-cri, and Verveine," said Chérie.

"We shall dash those aside who stand in our way," said the man on the balcony.

"We shall dance," said Mireille.

"We shall grind our heel upon their necks," said von Bethmann-Hollweg.

And the Grey Wolves roared.

CHAPTER III

CHÉRIE'S DIARY

This is August the 1st. In three days I shall be eighteen. At eighteen one is grown up; one pins up one's hair, and one may use perfume on one's handkerchief and think of whom one is going to love.

The weather is very hot.

Cécile tells me that she saw Florian Audet ride past this morning; he was at the head of his company of Lancers, and looked very straight and handsome and stern; like Lohengrin, she said. I do not suppose he will remember my birthday with all this excitement about manœuvres and mobilizing.

There is no news at all about Amour. We are very unhappy about him.

Later.—Claude has written to say that he is ordered to Mons and that there may be an invasion, and that whatever happens we are all to be brave. We were not at all frightened until we read that; but now of course we are terrified out of our wits. Every time the bell rings we think it is the enemy and we scream. (Motto—to remember. It is better never to tell any one to be brave because it makes them frightened.)

August 2nd.—It is very hot again today. We wished we were in Westende. How nice it was there, bicycling on the sand in one's bathing dress! One day I rode all the way to the Yser and back. The Yser is a pretty blue canal and a man with a boat ferries you across for ten centimes to Nieuport. Of course that day I did not want to go to Nieuport because I was in my bathing dress; besides, I had no pocket and therefore no money.

I do not seem to write very important things in this diary; my brother Claude gave it me and said I was not to fill it with futile nonsense. But nothing really important ever happens.

There is no news of Amour.

Germany has declared war upon Russia; of course that is important, but I do not write about it as it is more for newspapers than for a diary. Louise says Germany is quite in the wrong, but as we are neutral we are not to say so.

Later.—We are going out for an excursion this afternoon as it is Sunday. We are going with Frieda to Roche-à-Frêne, to ramble about in the rocks, and Fritz is to follow us with a hamper of sandwiches, milk and fruit. Loulou is coming too. It was Mireille who suggested it. She said she thought we had been quite miserable enough. Mireille is very intelligent and also pretty, except that her hair does not curl.

Evening, late.—As nothing important has happened today—except one thing —I will write in this diary about the excursion.

(The important thing is that I saw Florian, and that he says he will come to my birthday party.) But now about the excursion. We were almost cheerful after being so wretched and frightened and unhappy all the morning about the war.

Even Loulou said that it was difficult to think that anything dreadful would happen with such a bright sun shining and the sky so blue. Frieda was sulky and silent, and kept dropping behind to be near Fritz. Loulou said that perhaps if Germany does not behave properly all the Germans will be sent away from Belgium. That means that Frieda would have to go. We should not be sorry if she did. She is so changed of late. When we speak to her she does not answer; when we laugh or say anything funny she looks at us with round, staring eyes that Mireille says are like those of a crazy cat that stalks about in the evening. I suggested that perhaps Frieda is in love, as I am told that it is love that makes those evening cats so crazy. It would be quite romantic and interesting if Frieda were in love. Perhaps if Fritz Hollander were not just a servant— Frieda is more of a *demoiselle de compagnie*—I should say that she might be in love with him. But he never looks at her except to scowl.

Today on our excursion I saw him do a funny thing. We came upon a spring of water hidden among the rocks, and while the others went on I stayed behind and clambered about, picking ferns. Fritz had also left the road, and was coming along behind us. As he caught sight of the water he stopped. He took a little notebook from his pocket, tore out a sheet, and having looked round as if he feared some one might be watching him, he scribbled something on the paper. Then he hurried back to the road and stuck the paper on the trunk of a tree. I thought it must be a love-letter or some message, so I slipped down the rocks and went to look at it. There were only two words written on the scrap of paper: "*Trinkwasser—rechts.*"

I found that very strange. We never thought he knew German. I wondered why he did it and was going to ask him, but when he saw me he looked so cross that I did not dare. Later on, as we rambled about in the wood we came upon another piece of paper stuck on a tree. "*Trinkwasser—links,*" was written on it. I told Loulou what I had seen, and she went straight to Fritz and asked him what it meant. He said he had done it for Frieda, so that she should know where to find water.

"She is a thirsty soul," he added, and he laughed, showing a lot of small, rabbity teeth. I do not think I have ever seen Fritz laugh all the time he has been with us; he does not look very nice when he does.

But—as Frieda says of his ears—I suppose he has the laugh God gave him.

The walk about Roche-à-Frêne was fantastic and beautiful.

After eating our sandwiches we lay on the grass and looked at the sky.

Perhaps I dozed, for suddenly I thought I was in Westende the day that the aeroplane passed above me as I swam far out in the sea. I heard the angry whirr of the engine, but this time it seemed to sound much louder than any I had ever heard.

I opened my eyes and there it was, above us, flying very high and looking for all the world like a beetle. It was all white except for a panel of sky-blue painted across the centre of each wing. I noticed that its wings were not straight as all the others I have seen, but sweeping backwards like those of a bird. I called out to the others, and Mireille said—

"How lovely it is! Like a white beetle with blue under its wings!"

Then an extraordinary thing happened. Fritz, who had been sitting some distance off looking at a paper, leaped to his feet as if he had been shot. He is short-sighted, and his glasses dropped off his nose into the grass.

"My glasses, my glasses!" he cried out, as if he were quite off his head. And Frieda actually ran to look for them, just as if she were his servant. "What did she say?" Fritz was crying; "like a beetle? white? with blue under its wings?" Frieda kept looking up and saying, "*Ja! ja! ja!*" and Fritz was calling for his glasses. They both seemed demented. The scarab-like aeroplane whirred out of sight.

Loulou had got up and was very pale. She made us go home at once and never spoke all the way.

It was when we were passing through Suzaine that we met Florian. He was on horseback. I did not think he looked like Lohengrin, but more like Charles le Téméraire, or the Cid, el Campeador.

He told us—and his horse kept prancing and dancing about while he spoke— that his regiment was encamped on the banks of the Meuse awaiting orders. They might be sent to the frontier at any moment. But, unless that happened, he said he would make a point of coming to see us on the 4th—even if he could only get an hour's leave. I reminded him that he had never missed coming to see us on that day since the very first birthday I had in Claude's house, when I was eight years old and my father and mother had just died in Namur.

Loulou always tells me that I was like a little wild thing, shrinking and trembling and weeping in my black dress, and afraid of everybody. On that particular birthday I wept so much that my brother Claude had the idea of sending for Florian—who is his godson—and asking him to try and make friends with me. I remember Florian coming into the room—this very room that I am writing in now—a boy of fourteen with short curly hair and very clear steely-blue eyes. A little like André but better-looking. He was what Loulou calls "tres-crâne." "Bonjour," he said to me in his firm, clear voice. "My name is Florian. I hate girls." I thought that rather a funny thing to say, so I stopped crying and gave a little laugh. "Girls," Florian continued, looking at me with disapproval, "are always either moping or giggling."

I stopped giggling at once; and I also left off moping so as not to be hated by Florian.

All these thoughts passed through my head as I watched him bending down and talking to Loulou very quickly and earnestly, while his horse was dancing about sideways all over the road. He certainly looked like a very young Charles le Téméraire or like the knight who went to waken la Belle au Bois dormant.

August 3rd.—We are very happy. Amour is safe! He is in the care of the station-master at Marché and André is going very early tomorrow morning to fetch him. André says that fetching dogs is not exactly a Service Militaire, but it is in the line of a Scout's work to sally forth in subservience to ladies' wishes, and obey their behests. He said he would wear Mireille's colours, and she gave him the crumpled Scotch ribbon from the bottom of her plait.

We have invited Lucile, Jeannette, Cécile and Cri-cri, to come tomorrow evening. It will not be a real birthday party with dancing as it was last year, because everything is uncomfortable and unsettled owing to the Germans behaving so badly. However neutral one may be, one cannot help being very disgusted with them. Even Frieda had a hang-dog air today when Loulou read out loud that the Germans had actually sent a note to our King proposing that he should let them march through our country to get at France! Of course our King has said No. And we all went out to the Place de l'Église to cheer for him this afternoon. It was André who came to tell us that all Bomal was going.

It was beautiful and every one was very enthusiastic. The Bourgmestre made a speech; then we sang la Brabançonne and the dear old Curé invoked a blessing on our land and on our King. We all waved handkerchiefs and some people wept. Marie and Mariette came too, but Frieda hid in the house, being ashamed of her country, as she may well be.

Fritz was there, and Mariette remarked that he seemed to be the only young man left in Bomal. It is true. All the others have either been called to military service or have gone as volunteers. The Square today was full of girls and children and quite old people.

I felt rather pleased that Fritz belongs to us. "A man in the house gives one a sense of security," said Loulou the other day. I reminded her of it as we were coming home, but she seemed worried and unhappy. "Since your brother has left," she said, "Fritz is very much changed. He does not behave like a servant; he never asks for my orders. Yesterday at Roche-à-Frêne he was like a lunatic. And so was Frieda." Poor Loulou looked very white as she said this, and added that she wished Claude would come back.

There is certainly something curious about Fritz. This evening he brought us the paper and stood looking at us while we opened it. I read over Loulou's shoulder that the Germans had marched into the Grand-duchy of Luxembourg and taken possession of the railways as if the place belonged to them. When I raised my eyes I saw Fritz staring at us and he had his hands in his pockets. He took them out when Loulou looked up and spoke to him.

She said, "Fritz, this is dreadful news"; and he said, "Yes, madam," and smiled that curious rabbity smile of his.

"Tell me," said Loulou, "did the master say anything to you when you saw him to the train the other night?"

"Yes, madam," said Fritz.

"What—what did he say?" asked Loulou very anxiously.

Fritz waited a long time before he answered. "The master said"—and he smiled that horrible smile again,—"the master said I was to protect you in case *those dogs* came here. That's what he said—those dogs! Those dogs—" he repeated, glaring at Loulou and at me until we felt quite strange and sick.

Little Mireille had just come into the room, and she asked somewhat anxiously, "What dogs are you talking about?"

Fritz wheeled round on her with a savage look. "German dogs," said he. "And they bite."

Nobody spoke for a moment. Then Loulou sighed. "Who would have conceived it possible a month ago!" she murmured. "Why, even ten days ago, no one dreamed of war."

Fritz took a step forward. "Some of us have been dreaming of war," he said—and there was something in his tone that made Loulou look up at him with startled eyes,—"dreaming of war, not for the past ten days, but for the past ten years." He rolled his eyes at us; then he turned on his heel and strode out of the room.

Loulou has written a long letter to Claude. But will it reach him?

CHAPTER IV

Mireille's Diary

This is an important day, August the 4th—Chérie's birthday. Loulou has given her a gold watch and a sky-blue chiffon scarf; and I gave her a box of chocolates—almost full!—and a rubber face that makes grimaces according to how you squeeze it, and also a money-box in the shape of an elephant that bobs its head when you put money in it and keeps on bobbing for quite a long time afterwards; Cécile and Jeannette sent roses, Lucile and Cri-cri a box of fondants, and Verveine Mellot, from whom we never expected anything, sent a parasol. We had not invited Verveine for tonight because she lives so far away, quite out of the village; but we shall do so now because of the parasol.

We nearly had no party at all, Maman and Chérie being worried about the Germans. But I cried, and they hate to see me cry, so they said that just those five girls whom we see every day were not really a party at all and they might come.

The great event of today has been that Amour has arrived in his basket, with 14 francs to pay on him; we were very glad, and Chérie said it was just like receiving a new dog as a birthday present. André was not able to bring Amour himself because he had been sent on some other Service Militaire in a great hurry on his motorcycle. The one drawback about Amour has been that he took the rubber face in his mouth and would not drop it and hid with it. We found it afterwards under the bed, but most of the colours had been licked off and Mariette says it is permanently distorted.

Mariette and Marie are going away today. They are taking only a few things and are going to Liège, where they say they will feel safer. Marie said we ought to go too, and Maman answered that if things went on like this we certainly should. Maman has cried a good deal today; and Frieda is shamming sick and has locked herself in her room. We have not seen Fritz since last night. Altogether everything is very fearful and exciting. Dinner is going to be like a picnic with nothing much to eat; but there are cakes and sweets and little curly sandwiches, all beautifully arranged with flowers, on the long table for this evening; and we shall drink orangeade and grenadine. We were to have had ices as well, but the pâtissier has joined the army and his wife has too many children and is so miserable that she will not make ices. She told us that her husband and other soldiers were digging ditches all round Belgium to prevent the Germans from coming in.

Now I am going to dress. I shall wear pink, and Chérie will be all in white like a bride. She will have her hair up for the first time, done all in curls and whirligigs, to look like that cake Frieda calls *Kugelhopf.*

Maman is going to make herself pretty too. She has promised not to think of war or of the Germans until tomorrow morning because, as Chérie said, one is eighteen only once in one's life. Now I come to think of it, one is also eleven only once in one's life. I shall remember to say that when my next birthday comes....

———————————————————

While Mireille sat in the little study writing her diary with exceeding care, her head very much on one side and the tip of her tongue moving slowly from one side of her half-open mouth to the other, the door was opened and Fritz looked into the room. He shut the door again, and having listened for a moment on the landing to the soft-murmuring voices of Louise and Chérie, he went upstairs to the second floor and turned the handle of Frieda's door. It was locked.

"Open the door," he said.

Frieda obeyed. It was not the first time that she opened her door to Fritz.

"How loud you speak," she murmured, locking and bolting the door again, "they may hear you."

"I don't care if they do," said Fritz, sitting down and lighting a cigarette. "For two years I have played the servant. Tomorrow I shall be the master."

"Tomorrow!" gasped Frieda. "Is it—as near as all that?"

"Nearer, perhaps," murmured Fritz looking out of the window at the crimsoning western sky. The round red August sun had set, but the day still lingered, as if loth to end. Where the sky was lightest it bore on its breast the colourless crescent of the moon, like a pale wound by which the day must die.

"Nearer, perhaps," repeated Fritz. "Be ready to leave."

———————————————————

That day the storm had already broken over Europe. The Grey Wolves were pouring into Belgium from the south-east. At Dohain, at Francorchamps, at Stavelot the grey line rolled in, wave on wave, and in their wake came violence and death.

But the guns were not speaking yet. In the village of Bomal, a bare twenty miles away, nobody knew of it; and Louise, fastening a rose in Chérie's shining tresses said, "We will think of the war tomorrow."

Chérie kissed her and smiled. She smiled somewhat wistfully, and gazed at her own lovely reflection in the mirror. The hot blue day had faded into a gentle blue evening and Florian Audet had not kept his promise. Perhaps, thought Chérie, his regiment has received orders to leave their encampment on the Meuse; perhaps he has been sent to the frontier, but still—and she sighed—she would have loved to have seen him and bidden him good-bye....

But now little Mireille in her pink frock, looking like a blossom blown from a peach-tree, came running in to call her. The door-bell had rung and there was no one to answer it, since Marie and Mariette had gone and Frieda was locked in her room and Fritz had vanished. So the two ran lightly downstairs and opened the door to Lucile and Cri-cri, radiant in pale blue muslin; and soon Cécile and Jeannette and Verveine arrived too, and they all tripped into the drawing-room with light skirts swinging and buoyant curls afloat.

Verveine sat at the piano and the others danced and sang.

Sur le pont
D'Avignon
On y danse
On y danse,
Sur le pont
D'Avignon
On y danse
Tout en rond!

The laughing treble voices could be heard through the windows, thrown wide open to the mild evening air, and a young soldier on horseback galloping through the quiet village heard the song before he pulled up at Dr. Brandès's door. It was Florian Audet keeping his promise.

He slipped his bridle over the little iron gate and rang the bell. Louise herself came down and opened the door to him.

"Ah, Florian! How glad Chérie will be!" she exclaimed. Then, as the light from the hall beat full on his set face, "Why, how pale you are!" she cried.

"I must speak to you," said Florian drawing her into the doctor's surgery and shutting the door.

Louise felt her heart drop like a stone within her. "Is there worse news?"

"The worst possible," said Florian. Then his eyes wandered over the pretty, helpless figure before him. "Why are you dressed up like this?" he asked harshly.

"Why, Florian …" stammered Louise, "it is Chérie's birthday … and…."

Sur le pont
D'Avignon
On y danse
On y danse,

sang the girlish voices upstairs.

Florian turned away with a groan. "What shall I do?" he muttered. "What will be the end of it?" Turning he saw Louise's stricken eyes gazing at him, and he took her hand. "Marraine," he said, "you will be very brave—it is best that I should tell you——"

"Yes, Florian," said Louise, and the colour ebbed slowly from her face, leaving it as white as milk.

"The country is invaded at all points. There has been fighting at Verviers…."

"At Verviers!" gasped Louise, and her large eyes were like inkblots in her colourless face.

"Yes, and at Fleron."

There was silence. Then Louise spoke. "What—what will happen to us? What does it mean ... to our country?"

"It means ruin and butchery," muttered Florian through his clenched teeth; "it means violence, carnage, and devastation." Then he walked up and down the room. "We are holding Visé," he muttered, "we are holding it against Von Emmich's hell-hounds. And when we cannot hold it any longer we will blow up the bridge on the Meuse."

Louise had sunk into a chair. For a few moments neither spoke. Then Louise looked up.

"Will they—is it likely that they will come here?"

"They may," said Florian gravely, and as he looked at her and thought of her alone in the house with Chérie and Mireille a spasm crossed his face and tightened his lips.

"Will you be with us?" asked Louise, gazing at his stalwart figure and strong clenched hands. "How long can you stay here?"

"Forty minutes," replied Florian bitterly.

Again there was silence. Then he said, "What about that Dutchman— Claude's servant? Where is he?"

"Fritz?" said Louise, trembling. Then she told him what had taken place the night before, and also the events at Roche-à-Frêne. Florian listened to her with grim face. Then he strode up and down the room again in silence.

"Well," he said at last, "you have promised to be brave. You must listen to what I tell you and obey me."

He gave her brief, precise instructions. They were to pack their few most valuable possessions at once, and leave for Bomal early next morning for Brussels, via Marché and Namur—not Liège. "Remember," he added, "not Liège." If no trains were available they must hire a carriage, or a cart, or anything they could get. If no vehicle could be found, then they must go on foot to Huy and thence to Namur. "Do you understand?"

Yes, Louise understood.

Why not start now,—this evening? he suggested. They could go through the wood to Tervagne——

Through the wood to Tervagne!... in the dark! Louise looked so terrified that he did not insist. Besides, he reflected, there might be Uhlans scouting in the woods tonight. No. They must leave at dawn. At three or four o'clock in the morning. Was that understood?

Yes, it was understood.

"And—and——" asked Louise, "what are we to do with Frieda?"

"Don't trust her. But take her with you if she wants to go. Otherwise leave her alone. Keep your doors locked."

"Yes."

"And have you got money?"

Yes, they had plenty of money.

"And now," said Florian, looking at his watch, which told him that twenty of the forty minutes had passed, "I should like to see Chérie."

"I will call her," said Louise; then, at the door she turned to question him with her fear-stricken eyes, "Shall I tell them—shall I tell the children of the danger that threatens us?"

"Yes, you must tell them," said Florian. "And send them to their homes at once."

"Oh, what will Mireille do?" gasped Louise. "What if she were to cry? What if she were to fall ill with fear?"

"Little Mireille is braver than we are," he said, smiling and putting his arm around her drooping shoulders. "Courage, *petite marraine*" and he bent over her with fraternal tenderness and kissed her cheek.

He was left alone for a few moments; he heard the singing overhead stop suddenly. Light fluttering footsteps came running down the stairs; the door opened and Chérie stood on the threshold.

He caught his breath. Was this vision of beauty in the floating silken draperies his little friend Chérie? How had she been transformed without his noticing it from the awkward little school-girl he had known into this enchanting flower-like loveliness? She noticed his wonder and stood still, smiling and drawing a diaphanous scarf that floated mistily about her somewhat closer over her pearly shoulders. Her limpid eyes gazed up at him with blue and heavenly innocence.

A shudder passed through the man as he looked at her—a shudder of prescient horror. Were not the wolves on the way already? Were not the blood-drunken hordes already tearing and slashing their way towards this virginal flower? Must he leave her to the mercy of their foul and furious lust?

Again the fearful shudder passed through him. And still those limpid, childish eyes gazed up at him and smiled.

"Chérie!" he said. "Chérie!" and with his hand he raised the delicate face to his, and gazed into the azure wonder of her eyes.

She did not speak. Nor did her lashes flutter. She let him look deeply into the translucent profundity of her soul.

"Chérie!" he said again. And no other word was spoken or needed.

The forty minutes had passed. There was a hurried leave-taking, a few eager words of warning and admonition; then Florian had run downstairs, spurs clinking, and swung himself into his saddle.

As he turned the prancing horse's head to the north he looked up at the windows. Yes; they were all there, waving their hands, clustered together, the blonde heads and the brown, the blue eyes and the dark eyes following him.

"Remember," he cried to Louise, "remember—at dawn tomorrow! You will leave tomorrow at dawn." And even as he spoke the unspeakable shudder thrilled him again. Was it a foreboding of what the morrow might bring? Was it a vision of what the tragic and sanguinary dawn had in store for those he was leaving, alone in their defenceless beauty and youth?...

At the end of the street he turned again and saw that Chérie had run out on to the terrace and stood white as a lily in the moonlight, gazing after him.

He raised his hand high in the air in token of salute. Then he rode away. He rode away into the night—away towards the thunderous guns of Liège, the blood-drenched fields of Visé. And he carried with him that vision of delicate loveliness. He had spoken no word of love to her nor had his lips dared to touch hers. Her ethereal purity had strangely awed and enthralled him. It seemed to him that the halo of her virginal youth was around her like an armour of snow.

Thus he left her, fragile and sweet—white as a lily in a moonlit garden.

He left her and rode away into the night.

CHAPTER V

The young girls in their muslin frocks and satin shoes sped homeward like a flight of startled butterflies. Did they dream it, or was there really, as they ran over the bridge, a booming, rumbling sound like distant thunder? They stopped and listened. Yes…. There it was again, the deep booming noise reverberating through the starlit night.

"*Jésus, Marie, St. Joseph, ayez pitié de nous,*" whispered Jeannette, and the others repeated the invocation. Then they ran over the bridge and reached their homes.

Louise, Chérie, and Mireille were left alone in the deserted house.

Frieda's room, when they went upstairs to look for her, was empty. Her clothes were gone. There were only a few of her books—"Deutscher Dichterschatz," "Der Trompeter von Säkkingen," and Freiligrath's "Ausgewählte Lieder"— lying on the table; and the plaster bust of Mozart was still in its place on the mantelpiece.

"She must have slipped out while we were talking with Florian," said Chérie, turning a pale face to Loulou, who gazed in stupefaction round the vacant room.

"She was a snake," said Mireille, slipping her hand through her mother's arm and keeping very close to her. "And so was Fritz."

At the mention of Fritz, Louise shivered. "I do not suppose Fritz has come back," she said, dropping her voice and glancing through the open window at the darkened outbuilding across the courtyard. "He is surely not in his room."

There was a moment's silence, and they all looked at those lightless windows over the garage. The thought of Fritz lurking there, waiting perhaps in the dark to do some fiendish work, was very disquieting.

"We must go and look," said Chérie. So holding each other very close and carrying a lantern high above their heads they went across the quiet courtyard up the creaky wooden stairs to Fritz's room.

Fritz was not there. But his trunk was in its place and all his belongings were scattered about.

"It looks as if he intended to come back," said Chérie; and they trembled at the thought. Then they went downstairs across the yard and into the house again. They were careful to slam the heavy front door which thus locked itself; but when they tried to push the bolt they found it had been taken away.

It was at this moment that the distant booming sound fell also on their ears.

"What was that?" asked Mireille.

Chérie put her arm round the child. "Nothing," she said. "Let us go up and pack our things." And as Louise still stood like a statue staring at the door with the lantern in her hand she cried, "Loulou, go up to your room and collect what you will take with you in the morning."

And Loulou slowly, walking like a somnambulist, obeyed.

How difficult to choose, from all the things we live among, just what we can take away in our two hands! How these inanimate things grow round the heart and become through the years an integral part of one's life!

What? Must one take only money and a few jewels, and not this picture? Not these letters? Not this precious gift from one who is dead? Not the massive silver that has been ours for generations? Not the veil one was married in? Not the little torn prayer-book of one's first communion? Not one's father's campaign-medals, or the packet of documents that prove who we are and what is ours?

What! And the bird-cage with the fluffy canaries asleep in it? Are they to be left to die? And the dog——

"Of course we must take Amour," said Chérie.

"Of course," said Loulou, going through the rooms like a wandering spirit, picking things up and putting them down in a bewildered manner.

A clock struck eleven. Mireille, still in her pink frock, had clambered upon her mother's bed and was nearly asleep.

Boom! Again that low, long sound, rumbling and grumbling and dying away.

"It is nearer," breathed Louise. And even while she said it the sound was repeated, and it was nearer indeed and deeper, and the windows shook. Mireille sat up with wide, shining eyes.

"Is that a thunderstorm?… Or the Germans?"

"It is our guns firing to keep the Germans away," said Louise, bending over her and kissing her. "Try to sleep for an hour, my darling."

Mireille lay back with her silken hair tossed on the pillow.

"Are the Germans trying to come here?" she asked.

There was silence. Then Chérie said, "I don't think so," and Louise added, "Of course not."

"But—might they want to come?" insisted Mireille, blinking to keep her eyes open.

"Why should they come here?" said her mother. "What would they want in this little out-of-the-way village?"

"What indeed?" said Chérie.

Mireille shut her eyes and thought about the Germans. She knew a great deal about them. Frieda had taught her—with the aid of a weekly paper from Munich called *Fliegende Blätter*—all the characteristics of the nation. The Germans, Mireille had gathered, were divided into two categories— Professors and Lieutenants. The Professors were old men, bald and funny; the Lieutenants were young men, aristocratic and beautiful. The Professors were so absent-minded that they never knew where they were, and the Lieutenants were so fascinating that girls fainted away and went into consumption for love of them. Frieda admitted that there were a few other Germans—poets, who were mostly dead; and housewives, who made jam; and waiters, who were sent to England. But obviously the Germans that had got into Belgium this evening were the Lieutenants and the Professors. Mireille nestled into her pillow and went to sleep. She dreamed that they had arrived and were very amiable and much impressed by her pink dress.

She was awakened by a deafening roar, a noise of splintering wood and falling glass. With a cry of terror she started up; then a flash blinded her, another roar filled the air, and it seemed as if the world were crashing to pieces.

"Mireille!" Her mother's arms were around her and Chérie had rushed in from her room with an ashen face.

"Loulou, let us go at once—let us go to the Bourgmestre or to the Curé! We cannot stay here alone!"

"Yes ... let us go ..." stammered Louise. "But who will carry our things?"

"What things? We take no things. We are fugitives, Loulou! Fugitives!... Quickly—quickly. Take your money and your jewels—nothing else."

"Quickly, quickly," echoed the whimpering Mireille.

"If we are fugitives," sobbed Louise, looking down at her floating chiffon gown, "we cannot go out into the world dressed like this."

"We cannot stop to change our clothes ... we must take our cloaks and dark dresses with us," cried Chérie. "Only make haste, make haste!"

But Louise seemed paralysed with fear. "They will come, they will come," she gasped, gazing at the shattered window; the throbbing darkness beyond seemed to mutter the words Florian had spoken: "Outrage, violence, and slaughter ... outrage, violence, and slaughter...."

Suddenly a sheaf of flame rose up into the sky, illuminating the room in which they stood with a fantastic yellow glare. Then a terrific explosion shook the foundations of the house.

Louise catching Mireille in her arms stumbled down the stairs followed by Chérie. They knew not where they were going. Another explosion roared and shattered the coloured staircase window above them to atoms, driving them gasping and panic-stricken into the entrance-room.

Did hours or moments pass? They never knew.

Now there were voices, loud hoarse voices, in the street; short guttural commands and a clatter of hoofs, a clanking of sabres and spurred heels.

"Let me look—let me look out of the window," gasped Chérie, tearing herself free from Louise's convulsive grasp. She stumbled to the window, then turned a haggard face: "They are here."

Mireille shrieked, but her piping voice was drowned by the noise outside.

"They will murder us," sobbed Louise.

"Don't cry! don't cry," wailed Chérie. "The gate is open but the door is locked. They may not be able to get in." But even as she spoke she knew the fallacy of that hope.

"Wait," she whispered. "They are trying the door." Louise had followed her to the window, clutching at the curtains lest she should fall. "Look, some one is trying to open the door...."

Louise bent forward and looked out. "It is Fritz...." she shrieked, and staggered back. "Fritz! He has opened the door to them!"

Now there was the tramp of many feet on the stairs, and loud voices and the clanking of spurs and sword.

As if the imminence of their fate had suddenly invested her with new strength and dignity, Louise stood up, tall and tragic, between the two trembling girls. She crossed herself slowly and devoutly; slowly and devoutly she traced the sign of the cross on Chérie's forehead and on Mireille's. Then with arms entwined they stood motionless. They were ready to die.

The door was kicked open; military figures in grey uniforms thronged the passage and crowded noisily forward.

They stopped as they caught sight of the three entwined figures, and there was an instant's silence; then an officer—a lean man with a grizzled moustache—

stepped forward into the room.

Those behind him drew up stiff and straight on the threshhold, evidently awaiting orders.

"*Tiens, tiens, tiens!*" said the officer, looking the three feminine figures up and down, from glossy head to dainty feet, and his grey eyes twinkled. "A charming tableau. You have made yourselves beautiful to receive us?" His French was perfect; his tone, though slightly contemptuous, was neither rude nor unkind; his eyes were intelligent and humorous. He did not look like a hell-hound. He did not evoke the idea of violence, outrage, and slaughter.

In a sudden reaction from the supreme tension of terror a wave of faintness overwhelmed Louise. Her soul seemed to melt away. With a mighty throb of thankfulness and relief she felt the refluent blood stream to her heart once more.

The man had turned to the soldiers behind him—two seemed to be junior officers, the other six were men—and gave them a short, sharp order in German. They drew themselves up and saluted. The two younger officers stepped forward and stood beside him.

One of them—a tall young man with very light eyes—held a paper in his hand, and at the request of his superior officer read it aloud. The older man while he listened seemed to be surveying the apartment, looking round first at one door, then at the other, then at the upper floors.

Chérie and Mireille were amazed. They who had learnt German with Frieda understood what was being read.

It was a brief, precise description of the house and its occupants. This was the house of Claude Leopold Brandès, doctor, and reserve officer, age thirty- eight, married. His wife, his child—a daughter—and his sister lived with him. There were twelve rooms, three attics, a basement; kitchen, scullery, wash- house, harness-room, stable. There was a landaulet, a small motor-car, and two horses; all requisitioned.

"*Das ist alles, Herr Kapitän.*"

"No other adult males?" asked the Herr Kapitän.

No. Nothing but these women.

Where had the man Brandès gone to?

He had left on the night of July 31st.

For the frontier?

No, for the capital, it was believed. "But," added the young officer casting a fleeting glance at the three women, "that will be easy to ascertain."

"Any one of ours here?" asked the older man.

"Yes. A certain Fritz Müller, of Löhrrach."

Chérie quivered and tightened her grasp on Louise's hand.

"Where is this Fritz Müller?" asked the captain, looking about him.

"Downstairs," answered the lieutenant. "He was the man who opened the door for us."

"Well, put him in charge of the billets and see that he provides for twenty men," said the captain. "Now, as for us——" he took the paper from the other's hand. He turned it round and looked at the plan of the house roughly drawn on the back of the sheet. "Let me see ... three rooms on this floor ... four on the next ... Glotz?" to the other and youngest officer standing silent and erect before him. "Come with me, Glotz. And bring an orderly with you." Then he glanced at Louise and Chérie. "Von Wedel"—the light-eyed officer stood at attention— "you stay here." The captain turned on his heel and marched up the stairs, followed by the second lieutenant whom he had called Glotz and two of the soldiers. The other four stood in the hall drawn up in a row, stiff and motionless as automatons.

Von Wedel shut the door in their faces; then he turned his gaze on the three women left in his charge. He moved slowly, deliberately towards them and they backed away from him, still holding each other's hands and looking up at him with starry, startled eyes. He was very tall and broad, and towered above them. He gazed at them a long time, his very light eyes roving from Louise to Chérie, from Chérie to Mireille and back to Chérie again.

"Well, turtle-doves," he said, at last, and laughed, "did you expect us?" The three pairs of startled eyes still looked up at him. "Is it really in our honour that you put on all this finery?"

He moved a step nearer, and again all three drew back. "Well, why don't you answer?"

Louise stepped a little in front of the other two as if to shield them; then she spoke in low and quavering tones—

"Monsieur.... I hope ... that you and your friends ... will be good enough to leave this house very soon.... We are alone here——"

"Permit us then to keep you company," said Von Wedel, and added, in a tone of amiable interrogation, "Your husband is not here?"

"No," said Louise, and at the thought of Claude her underlip trembled; she

42

looked like a child who is about to cry.

"Too bad," said Von Wedel, putting one foot in its muddy boot on a chair and leaning forward with his elbow resting on his upraised knee. "Too bad. Well; we must await his return."

"But," stammered Louise, "he will not return tonight."

"Won't he?" His insolent light eyes that had been fixed on Chérie during this conversation now wandered with effrontery over the charming trepidant figure of Louise. "Why, what an ungallant husband to be sure! And may I ask where he has gone to?" He tossed the question at her carelessly while he drew a gold coroneted cigarette-case from his pocket and took from it the solitary cigarette it contained. "Your man told me he had been ordered to Namur."

"No—to Mons," said Louise.

"Ah yes, Mons. Interesting town"—he tapped one end of his cigarette on the palm of his hand, "fine old Cathedral of St. Waudru ... four railway lines ... yes. Did he go alone?"

Mireille pinched her mother's arm.

"Don't say," she whispered.

The officer heard it and laughed. He took hold of the child's arm and drew her gently away from her mother's side. "*Na! sieh doch einmal!*" he said. "Are we not sly? Are we not knowing? Are we not diplomatic? Eh?" Holding her by her small arm he backed her away across the room, then giving her a little push he left her and turned his attention to the other two again. Louise had turned deathly pale, but Mireille, unharmed and undaunted, signalled to her from the other end of the room, signifying defiance by shrugging her shoulders and sticking her tongue out at the spruce, straight back of the enemy.

He now stared at Chérie again, and under his insistent insolent gaze she trembled like an aspen leaf.

"Why do you tremble?" he asked. "Are you afraid of me?"

"Yes," murmured the girl, drooping her head.

He laughed. "Why? I'm not a wild beast, am I? Do I look like a wild beast?" And he moved a step nearer.

Louise stepped in front of Chérie. "My sister-in-law is very young," she said, "and is not used to the attention of strangers."

"My good woman," replied Von Wedel with easy insolence, "go and find some cigarettes for me." And as Louise stared at him with an air of dazed stupefaction he spoke a little louder. "Cigarettes, I said. Surely in your husband's study you will find some. Preferably Turkish. Quick, my good soul. *Eins, zwei, drei*—go."

After a moment's hesitation Louise turned and left the room; Mireille ran after her. Chérie darted forward to follow them, but Von Wedel took one long stride and caught her by the arm. "*Halt, halt!*" he said, laughing. "You stay here, my little turtle-dove, and talk to me."

The girl flushed and paled and trembled. "What a shy dove!" he said, bending over her. "What is your name?"

"Chérie," she murmured almost inaudibly.

"What? *'Chérie'?*" he laughed. "Did you say that to me? The same to you, Herzchen!" He sat down on a corner of the table quite close to her. "Now tell me what you are afraid of. And whom you are afraid of.... Is it of Captain Fischer? Or of me? Or of the soldiers?"

"Of everybody," stammered Chérie.

"Why, we are such good people," he said, blowing the cigarette-smoke in a long whiff before him, then throwing the cigarette on the carpet and stamping it out with his foot. "We would not hurt a cat—nor a dog," he added, catching sight of Amour, who came hopping down the stairs limping and yelping, "let alone such an adorable little angel as you."

The dog came whining piteously and crouched at Chérie's feet; she bent down and lifted him up in her arms. He was evidently hurt. Von Wedel said "Good dog!" and attempted to pat him, but Amour gave a long, low growl and the officer quickly withdrew his hand.

Louise reappeared bringing boxes of cigars and cigarettes, which she placed on the table. Mireille, who followed her, caught sight of Amour in Chérie's arms and heard him whine.

"What have you done to him?" she said, turning fiercely on Von Wedel.

He laughed. "Well, well, what a little vixen!" he said. Then he added, "You can take the dog away. I don't like dogs." Chérie moved at once towards the staircase, but he stopped her again. "No, no; give the dog to the vixen. You stay here."

Chérie obeyed, shrinking away from him to Louise's side, while Mireille ran upstairs with Amour and took him to Chérie's room. She kissed him on his rough black head and patted his poor paws and put him down on a cushion in a corner. Then she ran down again to see what was going on. Amour left alone whined and howled in hideous long-drawn tones of indignation and

44

suffering. When a few minutes later Captain Fischer, followed by Lieutenant Glotz and the two soldiers on his round of inspection, came downstairs, he stopped on the landing.

"What is that noise? Who is crying?" he asked.

"The dog, sir," said Glotz, "whom you kicked downstairs before."

"Hideous sound!" said Captain Fischer; "stop it."

And one of the soldiers went in and stopped it.

Captain Fischer went downstairs, followed by Glotz. When they entered the room Von Wedel turned away from Chérie and stood at attention.

Outside the boom of the cannon had ceased, but there were loud bursts of firing in the distance, sudden volleys which ceased as abruptly as they began. The three officers seemed to pay no heed to these sounds; they stood speaking together, the captain issuing brief orders, Von Wedel asking a question or two, and Glotz saying "*Ja, Herr Kapitän—ja, Herr Leutnant*" at brief intervals, like a mechanical toy. Glotz was round-faced and solemn. He never once looked at Louise, Chérie, or Mireille, who stood in a corner of the room watching the men with anxious eyes.

"What are they saying?" asked Louise in an undertone.

Chérie listened. So far as she could understand they were making arrangements as to where they should sleep.

"Eight men are to stay here," she translated in a whisper, "four in the attics and four downstairs. They themselves are going somewhere else—wait! They are talking of the Cheval Blanc—wait … wait … they are saying"—and her eyes dilated—"that they can't go there because the inn is burning...."

At this point Von Wedel gave a loud laugh and Fischer smiled. Only Glotz's chubby countenance remained solemn, like the face of an anxious baby.

"What are they saying now?" asked Louise.

Mireille whispered, "They are talking about the *Pfarrer*—that means the priest."

"About Monsieur le Curé? What are they saying about him?"

At this point Von Wedel laughed again. "*Der alte Esel!... Seine eigene Schuld....*"

"What is that? what is that?" asked Louise.

"The old donkey … his own fault," translated Mireille.

"And now what?" The captain was bending down and looking at his boots.

Chérie interpreted. "He says he will be glad to get the mud and blood off his feet...."

"Mud and blood?" echoed Louise in a horrified whisper. "Surely not."

Mireille nodded. *"Koth und Blut*—that is what he said."

A wave of sickness came over Louise; she felt the ground heave under her.

Now Von Wedel was helping the captain to take off his tunic, drawing the left sleeve down with great precaution.

"He says he is wounded," whispered Mireille.

"But he says it is nothing; that his arm is only grazed," supplemented Chérie.

The coat was off and Captain Fischer was carefully turning up his shirt-sleeve. Yes; the forearm was grazed and bleeding.

The captain examined it very carefully, and so did Von Wedel, bending over it and shaking his head with an air of great concern. The captain looked across at Louise and beckoned to her with his finger.

"Come here, *Gnädige*, please;" and as she approached him he said, "Your husband is a doctor, is he not? Then you will have some antiseptic in the house. Lysoform? Sublimate? Have you?" Louise nodded assent. "Bring me some," he said. "And a little boiled water if you have it."

Louise turned without a word and left the room.

"She is very stupid," said Von Wedel looking after her.

"She is very pretty," said the captain.

Louise passed the soldiers who stood in the hall talking together in low voices. She went down the stairs feeling dizzy and bewildered. Would these men stay in the house all night? Would they sleep and eat here? Would they order her about, and ogle Chérie, and bully little Mireille? How long would they stay, she wondered. A week? a month?... She entered her husband's surgery and turned on the light. The sight of his room, of his chair, of his book, open on the desk as he had left it, seemed to wring her heart in a vice of pain. "Claude! Claude!" she sobbed. "Come back! Come back and take care of us!"

But Claude was far away.

She found the little blue phial of pastilles of corrosive sublimate; she poured some distilled water into a small basin and found cotton and a packet of lint for a bandage. Then she went upstairs again, past the soldiers in grey, and entered the sitting-room. It was empty.

Where had they all gone to? Where had they taken Chérie and Mireille? She stumbled blindly up the short flight of stairs leading to the drawing-room. There she heard their voices, and went in.

Captain Fischer was reclining on the sofa, still in his shirt-sleeves, with his boots off. Von Wedel and Glotz were at the flower-adorned supper-table prepared for Chérie's birthday party, and were eating sandwiches in large mouthfuls. Their grey helmets were on the piano; their belts on a chair. Chérie stood cowering in a corner near the door.

"Where is Mireille?" cried Louise; and Chérie replied, "She is all right. He"— indicating the captain on the sofa—"has sent her to fetch him some slippers." Her lips quivered. "I wanted to go with her but they would not let me."

"I feel as if we were in a dream," murmured Louise.

"Ah," cried the man on the sofa, catching sight of Louise, "here is my good Samaritan." He crossed the room in his stockinged feet and took the basin out of her hands. He looked round a moment uncertain where to put it; then he drew up a satin chair and placed the basin of water on it.

"*Gut*," he said. "And what have we here?" He took the little bottle from her hand. "'Perchlor. of mercury, 1.0 gramme.' That is right." He shook one of the little pink tablets out on his palm and dropped it in the water. "Now, charming lady, will you be a sister of mercy to a poor wounded man?" He bared his arm and sat down on the sofa again, making room for her beside him; but she stood in front of him, and dipping some pieces of cotton in the water she bathed the injured arm.

The door opened and Mireille came in with a pair of her father's slippers in her hand. When she saw her mother stooping over the man's arm her small face flushed scarlet. She flung the slippers down and, running to the corner where Chérie was standing, she hid her face on Chérie's arm.

"*Ei, ei, the* vixen!" laughed Von Wedel, taking another sandwich. "Now we want something to drink. Not these syrups," he added, pushing the grenadine and orangeade aside. "Let us have some champagne. Eh, Glotz? What do you say to that?"

"And some brandy," said Fischer. "This scratch is deucedly painful."

There was a moment's silence. Then Chérie, taking a step towards the door, said, "I will fetch some brandy."

"I'll come too," said Mireille.

"No, no, no, no," cried Von Wedel, catching hold of them each by one arm. "You two want to run away. I know your tricks! No. The vixen stays here; and the angel"—bending to gaze into Chérie's face—"comes with me and shows me where the brandy is kept."

"She shan't! she shan't!" screamed Mireille, clinging to Chérie's arm.

"*Donner und Blitz!*" exclaimed Von Wedel, "what a little demon. You just catch hold of her, Glotz, and keep her quiet."

Glotz, who had been sitting at the table eating silently, rose and dried his mouth on one of the beflowered tissue-paper serviettes. "I know where the cellar is," said he, "I saw it on my round with the Herr Kapitän. If the Herr Kapitän permits, I will fetch the brandy myself." And he left the room quickly, paying no heed to Von Wedel's murmured remark that he was a confounded interfering head of a sheep.

Louise had burst into tears when Von Wedel had told Glotz to hold Mireille, and although the captain patted her hand and told her not to cry she went on weeping bitterly while she bandaged his arm.

Von Wedel looked at her a moment and then turned to Chérie. "What relation are you to that weeping Niobe? I forget."

"Sister-in-law," murmured Chérie inaudibly.

"What? Speak louder. I can't hear," said Von Wedel, seating himself on a corner of the table and lighting one of Dr. Brandès's cigars.

"Sister-in-law," repeated Chérie faintly.

"Sister-in-law? Good." He puffed at the cigar. "And I'll be your brother-in-law, shall I? Ah, here is the wine!" he exclaimed as the door was thrown open.

But it was not the wine. It was another officer, dressed like the others in a grey uniform bereft of all insignia; he was very red and covered with dust and mud. He saluted the captain and nodded to the lieutenant, loosened his belt and flung his grey helmet on the piano where the others lay.

"Ah, Feldmann," cried Captain Fischer. "What have you done?"

"My duty," said the new-comer in a curious hoarse voice.

"*Der Pfarrer?*" … questioned Von Wedel.

The man nodded and made a grimace. "And that idiot of a scout-boy too. It was he who fired at you," he said turning to Fischer.

"It was not," said the captain. "It was an old man, from a window. Near the church."

"Oh well, I didn't see any old man," said Captain Feldmann. "And these civilians must be taught their lesson.... What have we here?" he added, surveying the table. "I am famished." And he took two or three sandwiches, placed them one on the other and ate them. "Beastly hole, this," he remarked, with his mouth full. "We needn't have come here at all."

"Oh yes, we need," declared Fischer very sternly.

"Well, we won't discuss that," said Feldmann. "And anyhow we are going on in the morning. I should like something to drink."

Chérie had flushed to the roots of her hair. She had grasped the one thing only —they were going on in the morning! At any cost she must tell Louise that wonderful news. And she did so rapidly, in low tones, in Flemish.

Louise, who had finished bandaging the officer's wounded arm, burst into tears again; this time they were tears of joy.

"What are these women?" inquired Feldmann, glancing around with his mouth full. "They look like ballet-dancers."

"That one," said Von Wedel, with a coarse laugh, pointing at Louise, "is the weeping Niobe; and that" indicating Mireille—"is the demon child. And this"—taking Chérie's wrist and drawing her towards him—"is my sister-in-law and an angel."

"And this is Veuve Clicquot '85," said Glotz entering with some bottles in his hand and stepping as if casually between Chérie and her tormentor.

The men turned all their attention to the wines, and sent Glotz to the cellar three or four times to fetch some more.

They wanted Martel; they wanted Kirsch; they wanted Pernod. Then they wanted more champagne. Then they wanted more sandwiches, which Louise went to make. Then they wanted coffee, which Feldmann insisted upon making himself on a spirit-lamp. They set fire to the tablecloth and to the tissue-paper serviettes, which they threw down and stamped out on the carpet.

Von Wedel sat down at the piano and sang "Traum durch die Dämmerung," and Feldmann wailed a chorus. Then Feldmann recited a poem. He was very tipsy and had to put one arm around Glotz's neck and lean heavily on Glotz's shoulder in order to be able to stand up and gesticulate.

"Liebe Mutter, der Mann mit dem Kocks ist da!"
"Schweig still, mein Junge, das weiss ich ja.
"Hab'ich kein Geld, hast du kein Geld,
"Wer hat denn den Mann mit dem Kocks bestellt?"

Great laughter and applause from Captain Fischer and Von Wedel greeted this; only Glotz remained impassive; with Feldmann's arm around his neck, his chubby countenance unmoved, his expression vacant.

For some time they paid no heed to the three women clustered together in the furthest corner of the room, except to stretch out a detaining hand whenever they tried to move towards the door.

"No," declared Von Wedel, leering at them through his light, vague eyes. "No. You don't leave this room. Not all three together. Only one at a time; then we're sure she'll come back."

So they clung together with pale bewildered faces, whispering to each other every now and then the comforting words, "They will go away in the morning."

But the morning was not yet.

When Captain Fischer suggested that it was time to go to bed, the others called him an old screech-owl; whereupon Captain Fischer explained to them at great length that military discipline did not permit them to call him a screech-owl. And he called Louise to witness that he had been called a screech-owl.

But now Feldmann was singing "Gaudeamus igitur," so the captain joined in too.

"Come along," said Von Wedel, lurching towards Chérie with two glasses in his hand; "come, turtle-dove, *Brüdershaft trinken!*" He forced one of the glasses into her hand. "You must drink the pledge of brotherhood with us. Like this"—and he made her stand face to face with him, pushing his left arm through hers and raising his glass in his right hand.

Chérie shrank back, seeking refuge behind Louise. But he dragged her forward and caught her by the arm again.

"Obedience!" he roared, scowling at her. "Now sing; '*Lebe, liebe, trinke, schwärme*'—and when I get to the words '*froh mit mir,*' we clink our glasses together."

"Please not! please not!" implored Chérie.

"*Froh mit mir*"—repeated he, glaring at her through his heavy lids. And he sang:

Lebe, liebe, trinke schwärme
Und erfreue dich mit mir.
Härme dich wenn ich mich härme
Und sei weider
      froh
       mit
        mir!

At the last three words he clinked his glass against Chérie's. "Drink!" he commanded in a terrible voice. "If you do not drink, it is an insult which must be punished."

With a sob Chérie raised the glass to her lips.

Louise was wringing her hands. "The brute! the brute!" she cried, while Mireille holding her mother's skirts stared wide-eyed at the scene.

Captain Fischer looked across at Louise. "My Samaritan," ... he mumbled. "My sister of mercy...." He rose and approached her with a stupefied smile.

Mireille rushed at him like a little fury. "Go away," she screamed, "go away!"

The Herr Kapitän took her not unkindly by the shoulders. "Little girls should be in bed," he said thickly. "My little girls are in bed long ago."

Louise clasped her hands. "I beg you, sir, have pity on us; let us go away.... The house is yours, but let us go away."

"Where do you want to go?" he asked dully.

"To our rooms," said Louise.

"You have no rooms; they are ours," he said, and bending forward he widened his eyes at her significantly.

Louise looked about her like a trapped animal. She saw Von Wedel and Feldmann who had Chérie between them and were forcing her to drink out of their glasses; she saw Glotz seated on the piano-stool looking on with fat, impassive face; she saw the man before her bending forward and leering suggestively, so close that she could feel his hot, acrid breath on her face. The enemy! The man with mud and blood on his feet ... he was putting out his hand and touching her——

She fell on her knees and dragged Mireille down beside her! she lifted up her hands and raised her weeping face to him. "Your children ... you have children at home ... your little girls are in bed and asleep ... they are safe ... safe, locked in their house.... As God may guard them for you, oh protect us! spare us! Take care of us!... Be kind—be kind!" She dropped forward with

51

her head on his feet—on Claude's slippers—and little Mireille with quick tears rolling down her face looked up at him and touched his sleeve with a trembling hand.

He looked down and frowned. His mouth worked. Yes. He had three yellow-headed little girls in Stuttgart. It was good that they were in Stuttgart and not in Belgium. But they were little German girls, while these were enemies. These were belligerents. Civilians if you will, but still belligerents....

He looked down at the woman's bowed head and fragile heaving shoulders, and he looked at the white, frightened child-face lifted to his. "Belligerents" ... he growled, and cleared his throat and frowned. Then his chin quivered. "Get away," he said thickly. "Get away, both of you. Quick. Hide in the cellar —no—not in the cellar, in the stable—in the garden—anywhere. Don't go in the streets. The streets are full of drunken soldiers. Go."

Louise kissed his feet, kissed Claude's slippers, and wept, while Mireille smiled up at him with the smile of a seraph, and thanked and thanked him, not knowing what she thanked him for.

"But—what of Chérie?" gasped Louise, looking round at the frightened wild-rose figure in its white dress, trembling and weeping between the two ribald men.

"You shall take her with you," said Fischer, and he went resolutely across the room and took Chérie by the arm.

"What? What? You old reprobate," roared Feldmann, digging him in the ribs, with peals of coarse laughter. "You have two of them! What more do you want, you hedgehog, you? Leave this one alone."

"You leave her alone, too. I order her to go away." Fischer frowned and cleared his throat and tried to draw Chérie from Feldmann's and Von Wedel's grasp.

"What do you mean?" asked Von Wedel, going close up to Fischer and looking him up and down with provocative and menacing air.

"I mean that you leave her alone," puffed the captain. "Those are my orders, Lieutenant—and if they are not obeyed you shall answer for it."

"You old woman! you old head of a sheep," shouted Von Wedel; "answer for it, shall I? You are drunk; and I'm drunk; and I don't care a snap about your orders." And dragging Chérie's arm from Fischer's grasp he pushed him back and glowered at him.

"Your orders ..." stuttered the intoxicated Feldmann, placing his hand on Fischer's shoulder to steady himself, "your orders ... direct contradiction with other orders … higher orders …" He wagged his head at Fischer. "The German seal must be set upon the enemy's country…. Go away. Don't be a screeching owl."

"And don't be a head of a sheep," added Von Wedel. "*Vae victis!* If it isn't you, it'll be somebody else. It'll be old Glotz—look at him … sitting there, all agog, *arrectis auribus*! Or it will be our drunken men downstairs. Just listen to them!…"

The drunken men downstairs were roaring "Die Wacht am Rhein." Von Wedel's argument seemed to carry conviction.

"*Vae victis!*" sighed Fischer, swallowing another glass of brandy and looking across the room at the trembling Louise. "If it isn't I … then Glotz … or somebody else … drunken soldiers…."

He went unsteadily towards Louise, who stood clutching at the locked door. "Woe to the vanquished, my poor woman … seal of Germany … higher orders…. Why should I be a head of a sheep?…"

BOOK II

CHAPTER VI

It is pleasant to sit in a quiet English garden on a mild September afternoon, sipping tea and talking about the war and weather, while venturesome sparrows hop on the velvety lawn and a light breeze dances over the flower- beds stealing the breath of the mignonette to carry back at nightfall to the sea.

Thus mused the gentle sisters, Miss Jane and Julia Cony, as they gazed round with serene and satisfied blue eyes on the lawn, the sparrows, the silver tea-set, the buttered toast, and their best friend, Miss Lorena Marshall, who had dropped in to have tea with them and whose gentle brown eyes now smiled back into theirs with the self-same serenity and satisfaction. All three had youthful faces under their soft white hair; all three had tender hearts in their somewhat rigid breasts; all three had walked slender and tall through an unblemished life of undeviating conventionality. They were sublimely guileless, divinely charitable and inflexibly austere.

"It is pleasant indeed," repeated Julia in her rather querulous treble voice. Julia had been delicate in her teens and still retained some of the capricious ways of the petted child. She was the youngest, too—scarcely forty-five—and was considered very modern by her sister and her friend. "Of course the Continent is all very well in its way," she went on. "Switzerland in summer, and Monte Carlo in winter——"

"Oh, Julia," interrupted Miss Jane quickly, "why do you talk about Monte Carlo? We only stayed there forty-five minutes."

"Well, I'm sure I wish we could have stayed there longer," laughed the naughty Julia. "The sea was a dream, and the women's clothes were revelations. But, as I was saying, England is, after all——"

We all know what England is, after all. Still, it is always good to say it and to hear it said. Thus, in the enumeration of England's advantages and privileges a restful hour passed, until the neat maid, Barratt, came to announce the arrival of other visitors. Mrs. Mulholland and her daughter Kitty had driven round from Widford and came rustling across the lawn in beflowered hats and lace veils. Fresh tea was made for them and they brought a new note into the conversation.

"Are you not thinking of taking a refugee?" asked Mrs. Mulholland. "The Davidsons have got one."

"The Davidsons have got one?" exclaimed Miss Marshall.

"The Davidsons have got one?" echoed Miss Jane and Miss Julia Corry.

"Yes, indeed," said Mrs. Mulholland somewhat acidly. "And I am sure if they can have one in their small house, you can; and we can."

"Refugees are all the rage just now," remarked Kitty. "Everybody who is anybody has them."

"Yes, but the Davidsons …" said Miss Marshall. "Surely they cannot afford it."

"They have dismissed their maid," explained Mrs. Mulholland, "and this poor Belgian woman has to do all their housework."

"Yes; and Molly Davidson says that she is really a countess," added Kitty, "and that she makes the beds very badly."

"Poor soul!" said Miss Jane.

"I certainly think," continued Mrs. Mulholland, "that the Davidsons of all people should not be putting on side with a foreign countess to make their beds for them, while others who have good houses and decent incomes simply look on. In fact," she added, "I have already written to the Committee in Kingsway offering hospitality to a family of two or three."

"That is very generous of you," said Miss Jane; and Miss Julia shyly patted the complacent white-gloved hands reposing in Mrs. Mulholland's lap.

"We had not thought of it ourselves, so far," said Miss Jane. "But if it is our duty to help these unfortunates, we shall certainly do so."

"Of course you will. You are such angels," exclaimed the impulsive Kitty, throwing a muscular arm around Miss Jane's prim shoulders and kissing her cheek. And Miss Jane liked it.

"How does one set about it?" asked Miss Marshall; "I might find room for one, too. In fact I should rather like it. The evenings are so lonely and I used to love to speak French."

Mrs. Mulholland, to whom she had turned, did not answer at once. Then she replied drily: "You can write to the Refugee Committee or the Belgian Consulate. The Davidsons got theirs from the Woman's Suffrage League."

Then there was a brief pause.

"But I hear that the committee is frightfully particular," she went on. "They don't send them just to any one who asks. One must give all sorts of references. In fact," she added, with a chilly little laugh, "it is almost as if one were asking for a situation oneself. They want to know all about you."

There was another brief silence, and then Mrs. Mulholland and Kitty took their leave.

To Miss Julia, who accompanied them to the gate, Mrs. Mulholland remarked, "The idea! Miss Marshall wanting a refugee! With her past!"

"What past?" inquired Miss Julia, wide-eyed and wondering.

"Oh," snapped Mrs. Mulholland, tossing her head, and the white lace veil floating round her sailor-hat waved playfully in the breeze, "when people live abroad so long, there is always something behind it."

She stepped into her motor, followed by the pink-faced, smiling Kitty, and they drove away to pay some other calls.

Miss Julia returned to the lawn with a puckered brow and a perturbed heart. Neither she nor her sister had ever thought of Miss Lorena Marshall's past; Miss Marshall did not convey the impression of having a past—especially not a foreign past, which was associated in Jessie's mind with ideas of the Moulin Rouge and Bal Tabarin. The neat black hat sitting firmly on Miss Marshall's smooth pepper-and-salt hair could never be a descendant of those naughty French *petits bonnets* which are flung over the mills in moments of youthful folly. Her sensible square-toed boots firmly repelled the idea that the feet they encased could ever have danced adown the flowery slopes of sin.

"I do not believe a word of it," said Miss Julia to herself, and later on to her sister. Miss Jane was indignant at the suggestion. "This village is a hotbed of cats," she said cryptically; and when the vicar looked in after dinner to discuss arrangements for a Church concert they confided in him and asked his opinion. Had he known Miss Lorena Marshall before she came to Maylands? Did he think she had a past—a Continental past?

The vicar thought the suggestions ridiculous and uncharitable.

"Of course," said Miss Jane, toying with her favourite angora cat's ear as he lay purring comfortably in her lap, "we are narrow-minded old maids." The vicar made a deprecating gesture. "Yes, yes, we are. And we like to be sure that our friendships are not misplaced."

"We are narrow-minded old maids," echoed Miss Julia. The two Miss Corrys always said that, partly in order to be contradicted and partly in that curious spirit of humility which in the English heart so closely borders on pride. For is not the acknowledgment of a certain kind of inferiority a sign of unmistakable superiority?

When we say we are a humdrum nation, when we say we are a dull and slow and stodgy nation, do we not in our heart of hearts think that it would be a good thing if other nations took an example from our very faults?

Even so when Miss Corry said, "We are narrow-minded old maids"—she felt with a little twinge of remorse that the statement was not altogether sincere. Did she really, in her heart of hearts, think it narrow-minded to abhor vulgarity, to shun coarseness, to shrink from all that might be considered indecorous or unseemly? Then surely to be narrow-minded was better than to be broad-minded, and she for one would certainly refuse to change her views. Was narrow-mindedness mindedness nowadays not almost a synonym for pure-mindedness?

And—"old maids"! Did she really consider herself and her younger sister old maids? Had they—just because they had chosen to remain unmarried—any of the crotchety notions, the fantastic, ineradicable habits that old maids usually get into? Did they go about with a parrot on their shoulder like Miss Davis? Or dose themselves all day with patent medicines, like the Honourable Harriet Fyle? Did they fret and fuss over their food, or live in constant terror of draughts and burglars? Certainly not. And—come now—did they really feel a day older than when they were twenty-two and twenty-five respectively? Or did they look any older?—except for their hair which, had they chosen, they could easily have touched up with henné or Inecto? Were they not able to do anything, to go anywhere? Were their hearts not as young, and fresh, and ready for love if it happened to come their way, as Kitty Mulholland's or Dolly Davidson's? Did not their elder brothers—the parson and the Judge— always speak of them still as "the girls"?

No. Miss Jane and Miss Julia Corry were not quite sincere when they called themselves "narrow-minded old maids," and accordingly they had qualms and conscience-pricks when they did so.

A week later the two sisters returned Mrs. Mulholland's call. They fluttered into the large drawing room full of the subdued murmur of many voices, and were greeted absent-mindedly by the busy hostess and effusively by Kitty. The Davidsons were there, quite unsuitably attired (remarked Miss Jane to Miss Julia; nobody wore satin at tea), and they were explaining volubly to a group of ladies how it happened that their Belgian countess-refugee had suddenly left them.

"First of all, she was not a countess at all," explained Dolly Davidson.

"And she was not even a Belgian," Mrs. Davidson added, in aggrieved tones. "I cannot understand the W.S.L. sending her to us. Why she confessed before she went away that she was a variety artist from Linz and could only speak German and Czech. We always thought the language she spoke was Flemish.

It has been a most unpleasant affair."

Every one was tacitly delighted. Mrs. Davidson had been giving herself such airs of importance with her countess, and now it turned out that she had been playing Lady Bountiful to an alien enemy from a Bohemian Café Chantant. One would have to be super-human not to rejoice. "How did you get rid of her?" asked one of the ladies, discreetly repressing her smiles.

"A villainous-looking man came to fetch her, late in the evening," said poor Mrs. Davidson, blushing. "They made a frightful noise in the hall, quarrelling or something."

"Then they both went upstairs," piped up Dolly Davidson; and pointing to her brother, a lumpish youth who at that moment had his mouth full of cake. "We sent Reggy upstairs to tell them to go away at once. But Reggy only looked through the keyhole and wouldn't come down again until mother fetched him."

"It isn't true," mumbled Reggy.

"Finally we had to send for the police," said Mrs. Davidson, with tears of mortification in her eyes.

Mrs. Mulholland confessed that she felt rather nervous about her own refugees who were expected at any moment. "I wish I could countermand them," she said; but her sympathizing friends all agreed that having asked for them she must keep them when they came.

They arrived the following day—an uninteresting woman, with two torpid boys and a thin girl of fifteen.

The boys ate a great deal, and the girl was uncannily intelligent. Since landing in England they had had it drummed into them that they were heroes; they had been acclaimed with their compatriots as the saviours of Europe; they had had speeches made to them apprising them of the fact that the gratitude of all the world could never repay the debt that civilization owed them. They therefore accepted as their due the attentions and kindness shown them. They ate jam at all their meals and asked for butter with their dinner; they drank red wine and put a great deal of sugar in it; they complained that the coffee was not good. They borrowed Mrs. Mulholland's seal-skin coat and Kitty's silk scarves when they felt chilly, and they sat in the drawing-room writing letters or looking at illustrated papers all day long. They spoke French in undertones among themselves and accepted everything that was provided for them without any undue display of gratitude. Had they not saved Europe? Would Mrs. Mulholland still have a seal-skin coat to her back but for Belgium? Had it not been for King Albert, would not the Uhlans and the Death's Head hussars be sprawling on the Mulholland sofa, eating the Mulholland jam, criticizing the Mulholland coffee? *Comment donc!*

And had they not themselves, in order to save Europe, given up their home and their business—a stuffy little restaurant (*Au Boeuf à la Mode, Épicerie, Commestibles*) down a dingy Brussels street?

The restaurant soon became a Grand Hotel in their fond reminiscences. *Le souvenir, cet embellisseur*, swept the sardine-tins, the candles, the lemons, and the flies from its windows, built up a colonnaded front, added three or four stories and filled them with rich and titled guests.

"What was the name of your hotel?" inquired Mrs. Mulholland. "We stopped in Brussels once on our way to Spa, and I remember that we stayed in a most excellent hotel—The Britannique, or The Metropole, or something."

"Tell them," said Mme. Pitou to her daughter Toinon who acted as interpreter, —"tell them the name of our hotel—in English."

"Restaurant to the Fashionable Beef," said Mademoiselle Pitou; and Madame Pitou sighed and shook her head despondently. "Hotel," she corrected, "not Restaurant. 'Hotel to the Fashionable Beef.' Toinon," she added, "do ask these people to give us *potage aux poireaux* this evening, for I cannot and will not eat that black broth of false turtle any more."

———————————————

CHAPTER VII

The craze for refugees cooled slightly in the neighbourhood after that. The first rush of enthusiastic generosity abated, and when friends met at knitting- parties and compared refugees there was a certain ægritude on the part of those who had them, and a certain smiling superiority on the part of those who had not. They were spoken of as if they were a disease, like measles or mumps.

"I hear that Lady Osmond has them," said Mrs. Mellon.

"Has she really?"

"Yes. And poor Mrs. Whitaker, too."

"Mrs. Whitaker? You don't say so."

"Yes, indeed. Mrs. Whitaker has them. And she feels it badly."

"I will run over to see her," said the sympathetic Mrs. Mulholland. "I am so fond of the dear soul."

But that very afternoon Mrs. Whitaker herself called on Mrs. Mulholland, at Park House.

"How do you do, my poor dear Theresa?" began Mrs. Mulholland, taking Mrs. Whitaker's hand and pressing it. "I hear——"

"Yes, yes," said Mrs. Whitaker rather fretfully, drawing her hand away. "Of course you have heard that I have them." There was a brief silence. "I must confess I did not expect quite such dreary ones."

"Dreary, are they?" exclaimed Mrs. Mulholland. "Is that all?"

"It's bad enough," sighed Mrs. Whitaker. "You have no idea what they are like. Three creatures that look as if they had stepped out of a nightmare."

But Mrs. Mulholland overflowed with her own grievances. "Do they borrow your clothes and use all your letter-paper and order your dinners?" asked Mrs. Mulholland, quivering with indignation. Her cook had just given notice on account of Madame Pitou going into the kitchen and making herself a *timbale de riz aux champignons*.

"No. They don't do that. But they sit about and never speak and look like ghosts," said Mrs. Whitaker. "When you have time you might drop in and see them."

"I think I'll run over with you now," said Mrs. Mulholland; "though I don't for a moment believe they can be as bad as mine."

She put on her garden-hat and her macintosh, told Kitty not to let the Pitous do any cooking in the drawing-room, and went out with Mrs. Whitaker. They took the short cut across the fields to Acacia Lodge.

"What language do they speak?" asked Mrs. Mulholland, as she proceeded with Mrs. Whitaker through the green garden-gate and down the drive.

"They never speak at all," replied Mrs. Whitaker; "and I must say I had looked forward to a little French conversation for Eva and Tom. That is really what I got them for."

They walked on under the chestnut-trees towards the house. Eva in trim tennis attire and George in khaki came to meet them, running across the lawn.

"I've beaten George by six four," cried Eva, waving her racket.

"That's because I let you," said her brother, shaking hands with Mrs. Mulholland and allowing his mother to pat his brown cheek.

"Handsome lad," murmured Mrs. Mulholland, and wished she had brought Kitty with her, even though the Pitous should profit by her absence to prepare their *tête-de-veau en poulette* on the drawing-room fire. "Where are ... *they*?" she added, dropping her voice and looking round.

"I don't know," said Eva. "I have not seen them all the afternoon."

"I have," said George. "They are in the shrubbery."

"You might call them, dear boy," said his fond mother.

"Not I," said George.

"I will," said Eva, and ran down the flower-bordered path swinging her racket.

"Sweet girl," said Mrs. Mulholland, following Eva's slim silhouette with benevolent eyes, and then gazing even more benevolently at George Whitaker's stalwart figure. "She and my Kitty should really see something more of each other."

Mrs. Whitaker threw a penetrating glance at her friend's profile. "Schemer," she murmured to herself. "Certainly," she said aloud. "As soon as George goes to Aldershot I hope your dear daughter will often come here."

"Cat," reflected Mrs. Mulholland. And aloud she said, "How delightful for both the dear girls!"

George had sauntered with his long khaki limbs towards the shrubbery, but Eva reappeared alone.

"They won't come," she said.

"What!" exclaimed Mrs. Mulholland.

"Why not?" asked Mrs. Whitaker.

"They don't want to," said Eva. "The tall one shook her head and said, '*Merci.*'"

"I am not surprised," laughed George, "considering they have been exhibited to half the county within the last three days."

"I'll fetch them myself," said Mrs. Whitaker sternly. Then she turned to her son. "George, you who are half a Frenchman after your visit to Montreux, do tell me—how do I say in French, 'I desire you all three to come and be introduced to a very dear friend of mine?'"

There was a brief silence; then George translated. "*Venny,*" he said.

"Is that all?"

"Yes," said George.

His mother was about to go when Mrs. Mulholland suggested: "Had we not both of us better take a turn round the garden, and casually saunter into the shrubbery?"

"Perhaps so," said Mrs. Whitaker.

And so they did. George followed them slowly, with Eva hanging on his arm. She was very fond and proud of her soldier brother.

They entered the shrubbery and saw seated upon a bench three figures dressed in black, who rose to their feet at their hostess's approach.

"Goodness gracious! how uncanny they look!" whispered Mrs. Mulholland, and added, with a smile of half-incredulous pleasure, "I believe they really are worse than mine."

The three black figures stood silent and motionless, and Mrs. Mulholland found herself gazing as if fascinated into the depths of three pairs of startled, almost hallucinated eyes, fixed gloomily upon her.

Mrs. Whitaker addressed them in English, speaking very loud with an idea of making them understand her better. They seemed not to hear, they certainly made no attempt to answer her amiable platitudes.

Mrs. Mulholland, moved to something like pity by their stricken appearance, put out her hand saying, "How do you do?" and two of them laid their limp fingers in hers—the third, whom she now noticed was a child although she wore a long black skirt, neither stirred nor removed her stony gaze from her face. There was an embarrassing pause. Then Mrs. Mulholland asked with a bright society smile—

"How do you like England?"

No answer.

"George, dear, ask them in French," said his mother.

George stepped forward blushing through his tan. "Um ... er ..." he cleared his throat. "*S'il vous plaît Londres?*" he inquired timidly.

He addressed the tallest, but she gazed at him vacantly, not understanding. The little girl stood next to her—the large tragic eyes in her small pale face still fixed on the unknown countenance of Mrs. Mulholland. She conveyed the impression that she had not heard any one speak.

George, blushing deeper, turned towards the third ghost standing before him, coughed again and repeated his question, "*S'il vous plaît Londres?*"

Then a strange thing happened. The third ghost smiled. It was a real smile, a gleaming smile, a smile with dimples. The ghost was suddenly transformed into a girl. "*Merci. L'Angleterre nous plaît beaucoup.*" That was in order not to hurt the "half Frenchman's" feelings. Then she added in English, "London is very nice."

"Oh," snapped the astonished Mrs. Whitaker, "you speak English?" and her tone conveyed the impression that something belonging exclusively to her had been taken and used without her permission.

"A little," was the murmured reply. The smile had quickly died away; the dimples had vanished. Under Mrs. Whitaker's scrutiny the girl faded into a ghost again. The two ladies nodded and moved away. George and Eva, after a moment's hesitation and embarrassment, followed them.

"What strange, underhand behaviour!" commented Mrs. Whitaker; "never to have told me she understood English until today."

"I suppose they were trying to find out all your family concerns," said Mrs. Mulholland.

A word that sounded like "Bosh" proceeded from George, who had turned his back and was walking into the house.

"I think they were just dazed," explained Eva. "They look almost as if they were walking in their sleep. I never even noticed until today that they were all so young. Why, the little one is a mere kiddy;" she twisted round on her heel. "I think I shall go back and talk to them," she added.

"No," said her mother. "You will stay here."

That evening when Mr. Whitaker came back from the City his daughter had much to tell him, and even the somewhat supercilious George took an interest and joined in the conversation.

"The ghosts have spoken, papa!" cried Eva, dancing round him in the hall. Then as soon as he was in the drawing-room she made him sit down in his armchair and kissed him on the top of his benevolent bald head. "And—do you know?—they are really not ghosts at all; are they, mother?"

Mrs. Whitaker did not look up from her knitting. But her husband spoke.

"They are the wife, the sister, and the daughter of a doctor," he said. "At the Belgian Consulate I was told they were quite decent people. My dear Theresa," he added, looking at his wife, "I think we ought to have asked them to take their meals with us."

"I did so," said Mrs. Whitaker, with some asperity. "I did so, although they do look like scarecrows. But they say they prefer having their meals by themselves."

"Then you must respect their wishes," said Mr. Whitaker, opening a commercial review.

"Just fancy, Pops," said Eva, perching herself on the arm of her father's chair, "the youngest one—the poor little creature with the uncanny eyes—is deaf and dumb."

"How sad!" said her father, caressing his daughter's soft hair.

"Did her mother tell you so?" asked Mrs. Whitaker, looking up from the grey scarf she was knitting.

"No, not her mother," explained Eva; "the other one told me. The one with the dimples, who speaks English. She is sweet!" cried the impulsive Eva, and her father patted her hair again and smiled.

"Her name is Sherry," remarked George.

"Oh, George, you silly," exclaimed Eva. "You mean Chérie."

"How do you know her name?" snapped Mrs. Whitaker, laying down her knitting in her lap and fixing stern inquisitorial eyes upon her son.

"She told me," said George, with a nonchalant air.

"She told you!" said his mother. "I never knew you had any conversation with those women."

"It wasn't conversation," said George. "I met her in the garden and I stopped her and said, 'What is your name?' and she answered, 'Sherry.' That's all."

"Queer name," said his father.

"My dear Anselm, that is really not the point—" began Mrs. Whitaker, but the dressing-gong sounded and they all promptly dispersed to their rooms, so Anselm never knew what the point really was.

After dinner Eva, as usual, went to the piano, opened it and lit the candles, while her father sat in the dining-room with the folding-doors thrown wide open, as he declared he could not enjoy his port or his pipe without Eva's music.

"What shall it be tonight, Paterkins?" Eva called out in her birdlike voice. "Rachmaninoff?"

"No. The thing you played yesterday," said her father, settling himself comfortably in his armchair, while the neat maid quietly cleared the table.

"Why, that *was* Rachmaninoff, my angel-dad," laughed Eva, and twisted the music-stool to suit her height.

George came close to her and bending down said something in an undertone.

"Good idea," said Eva. "Ask the mater."

"You ask her," said George, sauntering into the adjoining room, where he sat down beside his father and lit a cigarette.

Eva went to her mother, and coaxed her into consenting to what she asked. Then she ran out of the room and reappeared soon after, bringing with her the three figures in black. As they hesitated on the threshold, she slipped her arm through the arm of the reluctant "Sherry" and drew her forward. "Do come! —*Venny!*" she said, and the three entered the room.

They were quite like ghosts again, with pale faces and staring eyes and the rigid gait of sleep-walkers.

They sat down silently in a row near the wall, and Eva went to the piano and played. She played the Rachmaninoff "Prelude," and when she had finished they neither moved nor spoke. She wandered off into the gentle sadness of Godard's "Barcarole," and the three ghosts sat motionless. Schumann's "Carnaval" did not cheer them, nor did the "Moonlight Sonata" move them. When Eva at last closed the piano they rose, and the two eldest, having silently bowed their thanks, they left the room, conducting between them the little one, whose pallor seemed more spectral and whose silence seemed even deeper than theirs.

"Poor souls! poor souls!" growled Mr. Whitaker, clearing his throat and knitting his brows. "Theresa, my dear," to his wife, "see that they lack for nothing. And I hope the children are always very kind and considerate in their behaviour to them. George," he added, turning what he believed to be a beetling brow upon his handsome son, "I noticed that you stared at them. Do not do so again. Grief is sensitive and prefers to remain unnoticed."

George mumbled that he hadn't stared and marched out of the room. Eva put her arms round her father's neck and pressed on his cheek the loud, childish kisses that he loved.

"May I go and talk to them a little?" she asked, in a coaxing whisper.

"Of course you may," said her father, and Eva ran out quickly, just as her mother looked up to say, "What is it?"

"I have sent Eva to talk to those unhappy creatures," said Mr. Whitaker. "We must try and cheer them a little. It is nothing less than a duty. Poor souls!" he repeated, "I have never seen anything so dismal."

"I think we fulfil our duty in providing them with shelter and food," said Mrs. Whitaker.

"You think nothing of the kind, Theresa," said Mr. Whitaker.

"I do," asserted his wife. "And as for Eva, she is already inclined to be exaggeratedly sentimental in regard to these people. She is constantly running after them with flowers and cups of tea."

"Nice child," said her father, with a little tightening in his throat.

"She is not a child, Anselm. She is nineteen. And I do not wish her to have anything to do with those women."

"Theresa?" said her husband, in a high questioning voice. "Theresa. Come here."

Mrs. Whitaker did not move. "Come here," he repeated in the threatening and terrible tone that he sometimes used to the children and to his old retriever Raven—a tone which frightened neither child nor beast. "Come here."

Mrs. Whitaker approached. "Sit down," he said, indicating a footstool in front of him; and Mrs. Whitaker obeyed. "Now, wife," he said, "are you growing hard and sour in your old age? Are you?"

"Yes," said Mrs. Whitaker. "I am."

"Ah," said Mr. Whitaker, "that's right. I knew you weren't." And he laughed, and patted her cheek.

This was not the answer Mrs. Whitaker was prepared for and she had nothing ready to say. So the wily Mr. Whitaker went on, "I have noticed lately in you certain assumed asperities, a certain simulated acrimony.... Now, Theresa, tell me; what does this make-believe bad temper mean?"

Mrs. Whitaker felt that she could weep with rage. What is the good of having a bad temper when it is not believed in? Of what use is it to be sore and sour, to feel bitter and hard, in the face of smiling incredulity?

"With other people, my dear," continued Mr. Whitaker, "you may pretend that you are disagreeable and irascible, but not with me. I know better."

This simple strategy had proved perfectly successful for twenty years and it answered today, as it always did.

"I *am* disagreeable, I *am* irascible, I *am* bitter, and hard, and cross," said Mrs. Whitaker, whereupon Mr. Whitaker closed his eyes, smiled and shook his head.

"Don't keep on shaking your head like a Chinese toy," she added. "Anselm, you really are the stupidest man I have ever seen." And then she laughed. "It is dreadful," she added, putting aside the hand he had laid on her shoulder, "not to be believed when one is cross, not to be feared when one is angry. It makes one feel so helpless."

"You may be helpless," he said; "womanly women mostly are. But you are never cross and you are never angry. So don't pretend to be."

Now Mrs. Whitaker was tall and large and square; she was strong-minded and strong-featured; she was what you would call a "capable woman"—and none but her own inmost soul knew the melting joy that overcame her at being told that she was helpless. She raised her hand to the hand that lay on her shoulder again, and patted it. She bent her head sideways and laid her cheek upon it.

"Now, what's the trouble?" said her husband.

"The trouble ... I can hardly express it," she spoke hesitantly, "either to myself or to you. Anselm!" she turned her eyes to him suddenly, the eyes full of blueness and temper and courage he had fallen in love with in Dublin long ago. "I hate those three miserable women," she said. "I hate them."

"What!" cried her husband, drawing his hand away from hers.

"I fear them, and I hate them!" she repeated.

"What have they done?"

"They have done nothing," said his wife, with drooping head and downcast eyes. "But I cannot help it. I hate and fear them ... for the children's sake."

"What do you mean?" Mr. Whitaker was sitting very straight. The thin soft hair still crowning his brow was ruffled.

"The mystery that surrounds them frightens me," said Mrs. Whitaker. "I don't know where they come from, what they have seen, what they have lived through. I should like to be kind to them, I should like to encourage the children to cheer them and speak to them. But there is something … something in their eyes that repels me, something that makes me want to draw Eva away from them. I cannot express it. I don't know what it is."

There was a brief silence. Then her husband spoke. "A woman's instinct in these things is right, I suppose. But to me it sounds uncharitable and cruel."

Mrs. Whitaker rose to her feet, her face flushing painfully. "Are we called upon to sacrifice our daughter's purity of mind, her ignorance of evil, to these strangers? Is it our duty to encourage an intercourse which will tear the veil of innocence from her eyes?"

"I am afraid so," said Mr. Whitaker gravely. "How can our daughter have pity on human suffering while she does not know its meaning? True charity, Theresa, cannot be blind; compassion must know the ills it tries to heal. My dear, we are face to face with one of the problems—one of the minor problems perhaps, but still a very real problem—which this ghastly war has raised. Think for a moment, Theresa; how can our girls, who are called upon to nurse the wounded in body, and comfort the stricken in soul, live in the midst of puerile ignorance any longer? Painful though it may be, the veil you speak of, the white veil that hides from a maiden's eyes the sins and sorrows of life, must be rent asunder."

"It is cruel! it is cruel!" cried the mother.

"Yes. War is cruel. And life is cruel. But do not let us—you and I—add to the cruelty of the world. If our daughter must learn to know evil in order to be merciful, then let innocence die in her young heart, in order that pity which is nobler, may be born." There was a long silence.

Then Mrs. Whitaker raised her husband's hand to her lips and kissed it.

CHAPTER VIII

Eva had gone upstairs to the schoolroom, now transformed into a sitting-room for the refugees, and had knocked softly at the door.

No one answered and she stood for a moment irresolute. Then the sound of a sobbing voice fell on her ear, "Mireille! Mireille!" ... The despair of it wrung her heart. With sudden resolve she turned the handle and went in.

Under the green-shaded electric light a picture almost biblical in its poetic tragedy presented itself to her eyes. The youngest of the refugees, the child, with her long hair loosened—and it fell like golden water on either side of her white face—stood motionless as a statue under the lamp-shine, gazing straight before her, straight, indeed, into the eyes of Eva as she halted spell-bound on the threshold. Kneeling at the child's feet, with her back to the door, was the eldest one of the three, her long black garments spreading round her, her arms stretched upwards in a despairing embrace of that motionless childish figure; her head was thrown forward on her arm and it was her sobbing voice that Eva had heard. Standing beside her holding a little golden crucifix in her clasped and upraised hands, stood the other girl—the girl who had smiled— and she was praying: *"Sainte Vierge, aidez-nous! Mère de Dieu, faites le miracle!"* Unmoved, unseeing, unhearing the little girl they were praying for stood like a statue, her wide, unseeing eyes fixed before her as in a trance.

With sorrow and pity throbbing in her heart Eva slipped back into the passage again, closing the door softly behind her. After a moment's uncertainty she knocked at the door once more, this time more loudly. A voice answered timidly, *"Entrez."*

They were all three standing now, but the tears still fell down the cheeks of the eldest one, who had quickly risen from her knees.

"May I come in?" asked Eva timidly. "I thought I should like to come and talk with you a little."

The second one, who understood English, came forward at once with a wan and grateful smile. "Thank you. Please come," she said. And Eva entered and closed the door.

There was a pause; then Eva put out her hand shyly and stiffly to the eldest one; "Don't cry," she said.

Surely no other words so effectively open the flood-gates of tears! Even though they were spoken in a tongue foreign to her, the stricken woman understood them and her tears flowed anew.

"Loulou, Loulou, ne pleure pas!" cried the younger girl, and turning to Eva she explained: "She cries because of her child"—she pointed to the little spectre—"who will not speak to her."

"Is she really dumb?" asked Eva, in awed tones, gazing at the seraphic little face, dazed and colourless as a washed-out fresco of Frate Angelico.

"We do not know. She has not spoken for more than a month." The girl's gentle voice broke in a sob. "She does not seem to know us or to hear us." She went over to the child and caressed her cheek. *"Mireille, petite Mireille! dis bonsoir à la jolie dame!"*

But Mireille was silent, staring with her vacant eyes at what no one could see.

Eva stepped forward, trembling a little, and took the child's limp hand in hers. "Mireille," she said. The blue eyes were turned full upon her for an instant, then they wavered and wandered away. "What has happened to her? What made her like this?" asked Eva, in a low voice.

"Fear," replied the girl, her lips tightening. And she said no more.

"Fear of what?" insisted Eva, with the unconscious cruelty of youth and kindness.

"The Germans came to our house," faltered the girl; "they … they frightened her." Again her quivering lips closed tightly; a wave of crimson flooded her delicate face. Then the colour faded quickly, leaving behind it a waxen pallor and a deep shadow round her eyes.

"Were they unkind to her? Did they hurt her?" gasped Eva, and for the first time, as she gazed at that motionless child figure, her startled soul seemed to realize the meaning of war.

"No; they did not hurt her. They did nothing to her. But she was frightened" … her arm went round the child's drooping shoulders, "and because she cried they … they bound her … to an iron railing…."

"They bound her to an iron railing!… How cruel, how wicked!" cried Eva.

"Yes, they were cruel," said the girl, and a terrified look came into her eyes. She moved back a little, nearer to the other woman, the tall black figure that stood silent, looking down at the glowing embers of the fire. She had neither moved nor spoken since Eva had entered the room.

Eva continued her questioning.

"And were you frightened, too?"

"Yes. I was frightened."

"What did you do? Did you run away?"

"I don't know. I don't remember. I don't remember anything."

Such terror and anguish was there in the lovely girlish face, that Eva dared to ask no more.

"Forgive me," she stammered; "I ought not to have made you speak about it. Forgive me—Mademoiselle." She placed her hand timidly on the girl's arm. "Or may I call you 'Chérie'?"

CHAPTER IX

The mild September days swung past; the peaceful English atmosphere and the wholesome English food, added to the unobtrusive English kindness—which consists mainly in leaving people alone and pretending not to notice their existence—wrought gentle miracles on the three stricken creatures.

Not that Mireille found speech again, but Louise watched day by day with beating heart the return of the tender wild-rose colour to her child's thin cheeks, and saw the strange fixed expression of terror gradually fade out of her eyes.

Mireille never wept and never smiled; she seemed to wander in the shadow of life, mute, quiet, and at peace.

But life and joy came throbbing back to Chérie's young heart, in fluttering smiles and little trills of laughter, in soft flushes and quick, light-running steps. Louise, seated by Mireille at the schoolroom window, would let her work sink on her lap to watch the girlish slender figure of her sister-in-law darting to and fro on the tennis-lawn; she would listen amazed to the sweet voice that had so quickly attuned itself to English words and English laughter. And her soul was filled with wonder. How—how had Chérie so quickly forgotten? Had she no thought for brother and lover fighting on the blood- drenched plains of Ypres? How could she play and talk and laugh while there was no news from Claude or from Florian? While they might even now be lying dead—dead with upturned faces, under the distant Belgian sky! And how, ah! how could she have forgotten what befell, on that night of horror but a few short weeks ago?

As if some subtle heart-throb warned her, Chérie would turn suddenly and gaze up at the two pale faces framed in the window beneath the red and gold leaves of the autumnal creeper. Then she would fling down her racket and, leaving Eva and Kitty Mulholland and George—who were often her partners in the game—without a word, she would run into the house and up to the schoolroom and fling herself at Louise's feet in a storm of tears.

"Mireille!... Florian!... Claude!" The beloved names were sobbed out in accents of despair, and Louise must needs comfort her as best she could, smoothing the tumbled locks, kissing the flushed, wet face, and finally herself leading her out into the garden again. Mireille went lightly and silently beside them, like a pale seraph walking in her sleep.

It was not only to console Chérie that Louise smiled in those first days of exile. Hope, like a shy bird, had entered into her heart.

There was better news from the Continent; all Europe had taken up arms and was fighting for them and with them. There had been the glorious tidings of the battle of the Marne. Then one day Florian had sent a message.

It appeared on the front page of *The Times*, and Mr. Whitaker himself went up with it to the schoolroom, followed by Mrs. Whitaker, Eva and George. Florian said he was safe, and was in touch with Claude. He gave an address for them to write to if this message caught their eye.

Louise and Chérie embraced each other with tears of joy. Claude and Florian were safe! Safe! And would one day come over to England to fetch them. Perhaps in a month or two the war would be over.

Louise dreamt every night of Claude's return. She pictured his arrival, the sound of his footsteps in the garden, his voice in the hall—then his strong arms around her.... Ah! but then he would see Mireille! He would ask what had happened—he would have to be told....

No! No! Mireille must be healed before he arrives. He must never know—Never! She need not tell him. She must not tell him.

Or must she?

It became an obsession. Must she tell him? Why, why must she tell him? Why break his heart? No; he need never know—never! Mireille must be healed before he arrives. Mireille must be taught to speak and smile again. Mireille must find again the dear shrill voice of her childhood, the sweet piercing treble laughter with which to welcome his return. The laughter and the voice of Mireille! Where were they?

Had the Holy Saints got them in their keeping?

Louise fell on her knees a hundred times a day and prayed to God and to the Virgin Mary and to the Saints to give back to Mireille her voice. Perhaps Saint Agnes would help her? Or little Saint Philomena, who both were martyred in their thirteenth year. Or if not, surely there was Saint Anthony of Padua who would restore Mireille's voice to her. He was the Saint who found and gave back what one had lost. And to Saint Anthony she prayed, in hope and faith for many days; in anguish and despair for many weeks.... Then, suddenly, she prayed no more.

From one day to another her gentle face changed. The soft lines seemed suddenly to be carved out of stone. When she sat alone face to face with Mireille their eyes would gaze into each other with the same fixity and stupefaction; but while the gaze of the child was clear and vacant, the eyes of the mother were wild and wide with some dark horror and despair. Fear—fear —the mad affrightment of a lost spirit haunted her, and with the dawn of each new day seemed to take deeper root in her being, seemed to rise from ever profounder depths of woe and horror.

"Loulou! dearest! What is the matter? Are you ill?" Chérie asked her one morning, noting her lagging footsteps and her deathly pallor.

"No, darling, no," said Louise. "But—you?" She asked the question suddenly, turning and fixing her burning eyes on the girl's face.

"I? Why do you ask me?" smiled Chérie, surprised.

"Are you well?" insisted Louise. "The English boy told me"—Louise seemed hardly able to speak—"that the other day—you fainted."

"Oh!" Chérie laughed and shrugged her shoulders. "How silly of him to tell you. It was nothing. They were teaching me to play hockey … and suddenly I was giddy and I stumbled and fell. I am often giddy and sick. It is nothing. I believe I am a little anæmic. But I really am quite well. Really, really!" she repeated laughing and embracing Loulou. "I am always as hungry as a wolf!"

And she danced away to find "Monsieur George" and scold him for telling tales.

Louise's eyes followed her with a deep and questioning gaze.

CHAPTER X

The Curate of Lindfield had arranged a Benefit Concert for the refugees. It was to be held in the schoolhouse on the last Saturday in September, and the proceeds were to be divided among the Belgian refugees of the neighbourhood, to whom also complimentary tickets were sent. The two front rows of seats were reserved exclusively for them.

For weeks past the excitement among the amateur performers who had offered their services had been intense. Miss Snelgrove, the Whitakers' nearest neighbour, who was going to sing "Pur dicesti" and "Little Grey Home in the West," had been alternately gargling and practising all day, until it was often hard to make out which of the two she was actually doing.

Finally her throat became so sore that Mrs. Mellon, of "The Grange," had to be asked to sing in her stead.

Mrs. Mellon, stout and good-tempered, said she would do anything for charity; so the "Habanera" from "Carmen" was put on the program instead of "Pur dicesti" and the "Little Grey Home"; and Mrs. Mellon heroically untrimmed her best hat, so as to have the red velvet rose which adorned it to wear in her hair.

"But surely," said Miss Snelgrove, who had magnanimously gone to see her on the eve of the concert to ask how her throat felt—she herself spoke in a hoarse whisper—"surely you are not going to sing Carmen in costume, are you?"

"No, not exactly in costume," said Mrs. Mellon, trying the rose first over the left temple and then under her right ear, "but I think the dress ought to be suited to the song; don't you? I have had my black lace shortened, and have added a touch of colour … here and there…." Mrs. Mellon indicated her ample bosom and her portly hips. "A scarlet sash, and the red rose in my hair will be quite effective. I *had* thought of having a cigarette in my hand—as Carmen, you know—but Mr. Mellon and the vicar thought better not.

"L'amour est enfant de Bohêm-ah,
"See tew ne maim pah, jet'aim-ah"....

she warbled in her rich padded contralto, and the envious Miss Snelgrove felt her own small, scratchy soprano contract painfully in her overworked throat.

George Whitaker was to perform a few conjuring tricks which he had learned from a book called *Magic in the Home*. He had performed them innumerable times in the family circle, with great adroitness and success; but when the evening of the concert came round he vowed he would not be able to do anything.

"I know I shall make an ass of myself," he said repeatedly to every one, and nobody had time to contradict him. About an hour before they were to start he stood with Chérie in the hall, waiting for the others.

Chérie was wearing a white muslin gown of Eva's, which George knew very well, and which made him feel almost brotherly towards her. Mrs. Whitaker and Eva were still upstairs dressing, and Loulou had gone to put Mireille to bed, telling the maid in anxious maternal English to "wake on her, is it not?"

"I know I shall make an ass of myself," repeated George. "My hands are quite clammy."

"What a pity!" sighed Chérie sympathetically, shaking her comely head.

"Most awfully clammy. Just feel them," said George, stretching out to her a large brown hand.

"I can see that they are," said Chérie.

"Oh, but just feel," said George.

Chérie cautiously touched his palm with the tip of one finger. "Most clammy indeed," she said; and George laughed; and Chérie laughed too.

"Besides," said the conjuror, "I am nervous. I positively am. Heart thumping and all that kind of thing."

"Dear, dear," said Chérie.

George sighed deeply and repeated, "I know I shall make a hash of things."

He did.

His was the first number of the program, and when he appeared he was greeted with prolonged and enthusiastic applause. Things bulged in his back and things dropped out of his sleeves; objects he should not have had popped out of his pocket and rolled under the piano; flags appeared and unfurled themselves long before they should have done so and in parts of his person where flags are not usually seen.

His mother sat bathed in a cold sweat as he fumbled and bungled, and Eva kept her eyes tightly shut and prayed that it might finish soon. But it did not. The flags, which should have been the crowning patriotic finale of his performance, having appeared in the beginning of it, there seemed to the agonized George to be nothing to finish with and no way of finishing. He went on and on, stammering and swallowing with a dry palate, clutching a hat, a handkerchief, and an egg, and wondering what on earth he was going to do with them.

Chérie had watched him solemnly enough in the beginning, but when he caught her eye and dropped the egg something seemed to leap into her throat and strangle her. When a tennis-ball dropped from his sleeve and he had to crawl after it under the grand piano while the Union Jack hidden up his back slowly unfurled itself behind him, she felt that she must laugh or die.

She laughed; she laughed, hiding her face in her hands, her forehead and neck crimson, her slim shoulders heaving, while Loulou nudged her fiercely and whispered, "*Ne ris pas!*"

George, returning from under the piano caught sight of that small, shaking figure in the front row; his hands grew clammier, his throat drier.

At last the curate, to end the painful performance, started applauding in the wings, and the abashed conjurer turned and walked quickly away—with a rabbit peering out of his coat-tail pocket.

In the wings he met the curate, who tried to comfort him. "Don't you mind. It wasn't so bad!" he said genially, clapping George on the back. "That silly girl laughing in the front row put you out."

"Not at all, not at all," declared George. "It was that beastly egg. Besides," he added, "everybody ought to have laughed. I wanted them to laugh. It was intended to be a funny number."

"Oh, was it?" said the curate, somewhat sourly. "You should have announced that on the program. Nobody would have thought it to look at you."

But the next number was already beginning. Mrs. Mellon was on the platform clasping a fan in her gloved hands. The gloves were tight and white and short, and so were her sleeves, and between the two a portion of red and powerful elbow was disclosed. The rose was in her hair, the sash round her waist, her eyes flashed with impassioned Spanish vivacity. At the piano the timid, short-sighted Mr. Mellon took his seat, after a good deal of adjustment of the creaky piano-stool.

No sooner had he nervously started the first notes of the introductory bars than Mrs. Mellon's loud contralto burst from her, and with hand on hip, she informed the audience in French that love was a rebellious bird.

Mr. Mellon, who still had three bars of introduction to play, floundered on awhile, then turned a bewildered face to his wife and stopped playing. There followed a brief low-voiced discussion as to who was wrong—she asking him angrily why he did not go on, and he murmuring that she ought to have waited four bars. Then they began again; and once more Mrs. Mellon told every one that love was a rebellious bird. With Latin fervour, with much heaving of breast and flashing of eye, she declared, "*Si tew ne m'aim-ah pas —je t'aim-ah*," and the warning, "*Si je t'aim-ah prends garde a toe-ah*" seemed to acquire a real and very terrifying significance.

Again Chérie, who had listened with becoming seriousness to the opening bars, was seized with a fit of spasmodic laughter. The agitated Mrs. Mellon telling every one to beware of her love seemed to her to be the most ludicrous thing she had ever heard; and she bowed her face in her hands and rocked to and fro with little gasps of hysterical laughter.

Louise glanced at her and then at Mrs. Mellon; and then she, too, was caught by the horrible infection. Biting her lips and with quivering nostrils, she sat rigid and upright, staring at the platform, but her shoulders shook and the tears rolled down her face, which was crimson with silent laughter.

Mrs. Mellon must have seen it—were the culprits not in the first row?—and she looked disdainfully away from them; but her song grew fiercer and fiercer, her notes grew louder and higher as she soared away from the pitch and left poor Mr. Mellon tinkling away in the original key, about three semitones below.

The other refugees, sitting on either side of Chérie and Louise, turned and looked at them; the Pitou children began to giggle but were quickly pinched back into seriousness by their mother.

The next number on the program was a dance; a somewhat modified Salomé dance, performed by Miss Price.

When Miss Price ran coyly in with bare legs and feet, and a few Oriental jewels jingling round her scantily draped form, even Madame Pitou gave way completely, and had to let the little Pitous laugh as they would, while she, with her face hid behind her handkerchief, gasped and choked and gurgled. The convulsive hilarity soon gained all the refugees. Every posture of Miss Price, her every gesture, every waggle of her limbs, every glimpse of the soles of her feet—somewhat soiled by contact with the stage carpet—made all the occupants of the two front rows rock and moan with laughter. Those immediately behind them noticed it. Then others; it was whispered through the hall that the refugees were laughing. Soon the entire audience was craning its neck to look at the unworthy, thankless foreigners for whose benefit the entertainment had been arranged, and who were rudely and stupidly laughing like two rows of lunatics.

The unwitting Miss Price was just rising from an attitude of genuflexion with a rapturous smile and two black marks on her knees, when she caught sight of the Pitou boy writhing with silent merriment at the end of the first row. Her eye wandered along that row and the next one and she saw all the bowed and quivering figures, the flushed faces hidden in handkerchiefs, and the heaving shoulders.

Casting upon them a glance of ineffable disdain she walked haughtily with her bare legs into the wings. Mr. Mellon rippled on at the piano for a little while, then he, too, stopped and hurried off the stage at the nearest exit.

Behind the scenes the artists were assembled in an indignation-meeting. There were eleven numbers still to come, but no one would go on. It was proposed that the curate should go out and make a short but cutting speech; and he went half-way out and then came back again, not having anything ready to say. Besides the sight of the refugees still convulsed with laughter upset him. For their part his appearance and disappearance did nothing to allay their condition, now bordering on collective hysteria.

Finally, after rapid consultation in the wings, the good-natured Miss Johnson was prevailed upon to go out and sing the "Merry Pipes of Pan." She was not nervous and did not care whether the silly refugees laughed or not.

When she stepped out she saw that Mr. Mellon was not there to accompany her, so after a long wait she went off into the wings on one side, just as Mr. Mellon—wiping his mouth after a hasty refreshment—came hurrying in on the other.

Miss Johnson had to be coaxed and driven and pushed out again, and this so flustered her that she forgot most of her words and had to make a series of inarticulate sounds until she came to the refrain.

Here she felt safe.

"Then follow the mipes,"

she warbled,

"The perry mipes——"

There seemed to be something wrong with the words, but she could not get them right

"Yet, the perry perry mipes of Pan!"

"Gracious goodness," murmured the husky Miss Snelgrove to Mrs. Whitaker, who sat near her, "what a strident voice!"

"Yes," assented Mrs. Whitaker. "And what *are* the 'perrimipes,' I wonder?"

———————————

There was no denying it. The concert was a fiasco. Owing to the execrable behaviour of the refugees and the contagion of their senseless laughter, a kind of hysteria gained the hall and half the audience was soon in a condition of brainless and uncontrollable hilarity.

Every new number was greeted with suffocated giggles, sometimes even with screams of laughter from the younger portion of the audience.

The curate—who had himself been found holding both his sides in one of the empty schoolrooms—made a caustic speech at the close of the performance about "our well-meant efforts, our perchance too modest talents," having appealed mainly to the risible faculties of their foreign guests, and he had pleasure in stating that the sum collected was eighteen pounds seven shillings and sixpence.

The refugees slunk home and were treated like pariahs for many weeks afterwards; while the word "Concert" was not pronounced for months in the homes of Mrs. Mellon, of Miss Johnson, or of Miss Price.

———————————

CHAPTER XI

CHÉRIE'S DIARY

Loulou is ill, and I am very anxious about her. It must be the English climate perhaps, for I also do not feel as I used to feel in Bomal. I often am deathly sick, and faint and giddy; I cannot bear the sight of things and of people that before I did not mind, or even liked. Certain puddings, for instance, and all kinds of dishes which I thought so extraordinarily nice to eat when we first came here, now I cannot bear to see them when they are brought on the table. Something makes me grind my teeth and I feel as if I must get up and run out of the room. And I have the same inexplicable aversion to people; for instance the nice kind Monsieur George Whitaker—I cannot say what I feel when he comes near to me; a sort of shuddering terror that makes me turn away so as not to see him. I cannot bear to look at his strong brown hands with the little short fair hairs on his wrist. I cannot look at his clear grey eyes, or at his mouth which always laughs, or at his broad shoulders, or anything.... There is something in me that shrinks and shudders away from the sight of him. Have the sorrows and troubles we have passed through unhinged my reason?...

But to return to Louise. I thought that what made her look so pale and wild was the anxiety of not hearing from Claude; but since his first dear letter ten days ago telling us that he is safe, she seems even worse than before. It is true he has been wounded; but that is almost a blessing, for the wound is not serious and yet it will keep him safely in the hospital at Dunkirk for months to come. He may remain slightly lame as he has been shot in the knee, but that does not matter, and he says his health is perfect.

Of course I thought Loulou would start at once to go and visit him, as she can get permission to see him and he has sent her plenty of money for the journey; but she will not hear of it. She only weeps and raves when I speak of it; and I do not think she ever sleeps at night. I can hear her in her room, which is next to mine, moaning and whispering and praying whenever I wake up. I have asked her why, why she will not go to see Claude—ah, if only I knew where to find Florian, how I should fly to his side!—but she shakes her head and weeps and her eyes are full of terror and madness. I ask her, "Is it because of Mireille? Are you afraid of telling him about her?" "Yes, yes, yes," she cries. "I am afraid, afraid of telling him what has made her as she is."

"But, Loulou, dearest, what do you mean? Was it not her fear that the Germans would kill us that took away her speech? Why should you not tell Claude? He would comfort you. He knows the Germans were in Bomal! He knows that they ransacked our house, that they killed Monsieur le Curé and poor André...."

"Yes, he knows that," answers Louise slowly with her eyes fixed on mine. "But he does not know——"

Then she is silent.

"What does he not know?"

She grasps my shoulders. "Chérie, Chérie. Are you demented? Have you forgotten—have you forgotten?"

Forgotten!... In truth, I have forgotten many things. There are gaps in my memory, wide blank spaces that, no matter how I try to remember, I cannot fill. Now and then something flashes into those blank spaces, a fleeting recollection, a transient vision, then the blankness closes down again and when I try to remember what I have remembered, it is gone.

I ask Louise to tell me what she means, to tell me what I have forgotten; but she only stares at me with those horror-haunted eyes and whispers, "Hush! hush, my poor Chérie!" Then she places her cold hand on my lips as if to close them.

I will try to remember. I will write down in this book all that remains in my memory of those terrible days and nights when we fled from home; when we hid starving and trembling in the woods, and saw through the trees our church-tower burn like a torch, saw it list over and crash down in a cloud of smoke and flame; when, crouching in a ditch, we heard the Uhlans gallop past us and saw them drag two little boys, César and Émile Duroc, out of their hiding-places in the bushes only a few yards from us.

We saw them—we saw them!—crush the children's feet with the butts of their rifles, and then taunt them, telling them to "run away!" I can see them now—two of the men standing behind the children, holding them upright by their small shoulders, while a third beat and crunched and ground their feet into the earth....

But stay ... the wide blank spaces in my brain go back much further than that.

What is it that Louise says I have forgotten? Let me try to remember. Let me try to remember.

I will go back to the evening of my birthday. August the fourth. Our friends come. We dance.

Sur le pont
D'Avignon
On y danse, on y danse....

Then Florian arrives—and goes. The last thing I see clearly—distinct and clear-cut as a haut-relief carved upon my brain—is Florian, turning at the end of the road to wave his hand to me. Then he is gone. I remain standing on the verandah, alone; I can see the row of pink and white carnations in their pots at my feet; Louise's favourite malmaisons fill the air with perfume, and the large white daisies among them gleam like stars in the grey-green twilight; I am wearing my white dress and the sea-blue scarf Louise has given me that morning. Then little Mireille's laughing voice calls me; they all come running out to fetch me, Lucile and Cri-cri, Verveine, Cécile and Jeannette....

Then, suddenly—the gun! the thud and roll of that first distant gun!...

The children have fled, pale, trembling, whispering to their homes, and we are left alone in the house; alone, Louise, Mireille and I, because Frieda and Fritz —wait! what do I remember about Fritz? That he is throwing our gate open to the enemy—no; it is something else ... something that frightens me more than that—but I cannot remember. I see Fritz laughing. Whenever I remember Fritz I see him laughing. He is leaning against a door ... there is a curtain.... I seem to see a red curtain swaying beside him and he is laughing with his head thrown back. What is he laughing at?... At me? What is happening that he should laugh at me? The blank closes round Fritz. He has vanished. I cannot hold him. It is as if he were made of mist.

But—before that; what do I remember before that?...

The guns are thundering, the windows shake ... a huge sheaf of flame rises up into the sky. There is a roar, an explosion; it is as if the world were crashing to pieces.

Then soldiers fill the house; officers take possession of our rooms—their coats and belts are on our chairs, their helmets are flung on the piano. There is a tall man with very light eyes....

A tall man with very light eyes....

Let me try to remember.

They order us about; they make Louise cry. One of them is wounded in the arm—I see it bleeding on the wet cotton-wool that Louise is binding round it —Now the blank comes.... I feel it coming down like a white cloud on my brain. Lift it, oh, holy Mother, lift it and let me remember!

There are two of the men near me; they blow their cigarette-smoke in my face; they want me to drink out of their glasses.... I weep ... I will not. They laugh and force me to drink. *Eins, zwei, drei!*—they threaten me with I know not what—the light eyes of one of them are close to mine ... impelling me, forcing me.... I am frightened, and I drink. Then they sing and clink their glasses together. I stand between them, and they make me drink again—cool frothing champagne and hot burning brandy—until I am so giddy that the floor heaves under my feet.

I cry and cry. I call Louise ... she is gone from the room. I see Mireille crouching in a corner staring at me, white and terrified. I call her—"Mireille! Mireille!" She springs up and rushes to me, she screams like a maddened animal, and the light-eyed man catches her by the wrists and laughs. The other man—one of the other men, I don't know how many there are—one who has red hair and has been reciting something in German, lies down on the sofa and goes to sleep. But another one—I remember his round face, I remember that the others were angry with him and called him names—he comes near to me and says something quickly in my ear. I am not afraid of him ... I know he is trying to help me ... but I am so sick and giddy that I do not understand what he says. He pushes me towards the door. He says in German: *"Geh! Geh! Mach' dass du fort kommst!"* and again he pushes me toward the door. But I turn to see what is being done to Mireille. She has a broken glass in her hand and she is trying to strike the tall officer in the face with it, as if she were trying to strike at his light eyes and put them out. There is a streak of blood on his chin but he is still laughing. He snatches up my blue scarf which is lying on the floor and he ties Mireille's hands behind her back with it. Then he winds it round and round her until she cannot move. Wait—wait—let me remember!... Then he takes one of the leather belts that are on the chair and he straps her to the railing—the wrought-iron railing that ends the short flight of steps that lead to the drawing-room. I see him lifting her up those three shallow steps, I see him kick over the china flower-pot on the top step in order to get nearer to the iron banister, I see him fasten her to it with the leather strap.... Her little wild face is turned towards me, her hands are tied behind her back. I hear what he says in German—he is laughing and laughing—*"Da bleibst du ... und schaust zu!"* Is he going to kill her? *"Schau nur zu! Schau nur zu,"* he repeats. What does he mean? Is he going to kill me
—to kill me before her eyes?

He comes toward me ... (the white cloud is coming over my brain again). I see the other officer—the one with the round face, the one who had tried to push me to the door—Glotz! yes, Glotz, that was his name—I see him dart forward and catch hold of the other man's arms—stopping him—keeping him away from me. I rush to Mireille and try to drag her away from the railing, to free her ... I cannot. My fingers have no strength. She is crying and moaning.

I hear Glotz shouting again to me in German—"Get away—get away!" He is struggling with the tall man to give me time to escape. I stumble up the stairs screaming, "Louise! Louise!" I fall, again and again, at almost every step, but I stumble on and reach her door—it is locked. Locked from the inside. But I hear sounds in the room—a man's hoarse agitated voice....

I stagger blindly on. I will go to my room, I will lock myself in there, and open the window and call for help....

I turn the handle and open my door. On the threshold I stop.... There is something lying there—a black heap, with blood trickling from it. Amour! It is Amour, with his skull crushed in.

As I stand looking down at it I hear a man's footsteps running up the stairs—I know it is the tall man—he is coming to find me! I stagger blindly forward, my feet slipping in Amour's blood. I draw the door after me. I rush forward and hide behind the curtained alcove where my dresses hang. The man stops at the door and looks in. He sees the dead dog on the threshold; he says "*Pfui*" and tries to push it aside with his foot. He glances round the apparently empty room, then he turns away and I hear him going down the passage, opening other doors, thumping at Louise's door, where the voice of a man answers him.... Then I hear him running upstairs to the top floor in search of me.

I slip from my hiding-place, I stumble again over the horrible thing that was Amour, and I rush down the stairs and into the drawing-room. Mireille is still there, tied to the banister, her face thrown back, the tears streaming from her eyes. She is alone, but for the red-haired officer asleep and snoring on the sofa. A thought has come to me. I cross the room, which swims round me, and I go to the sideboard—I take the bottle of corrosive sublimate from the shelf where Louise had put it—I open it and shake some of the little pink tablets into my hand—then I run to the table where the wine-glasses stand. One of them is still half-filled with champagne. I drop the tablets into it. Even as I do so I hear the man coming downstairs. He appears on the top of the short flight, near Mireille, and laughs as he sees me. "Ha, ha! the dovelet who tried to escape!"

I smile up at him. I smile, moving back towards that side of the table where his wine-glass stands. He passes his hand over his forehead and hair; his face is hot; I know he is going to drink again. Then he lurches towards me; he puts one hand round my waist and with the other grasps the glass on the table.... Now this again I see, clear-cut in my memory as if carved into it with a knife; the tall man standing beside me raising the wine-glass to his lips....

He stops—he looks down into the glass. His face is motionless, expressionless. He merely stares at the little bright pink heap at the bottom of the glass from which spiral streaks of colour slowly curl up and tint the pale-gold wine.

For what seems to me hours or eternities he stares at the glass; then his light eyes turn slowly upon me. And this is the last thing I see.

I carry the gaze of those light eyes with me as I slip suddenly into unconsciousness. I hear a crash—is it the glass that has fallen?... I feel the grasp of two strong hot hands on my arms—is he holding me, or crushing me down? I hear Mireille shriek as I try madly to beat back the enveloping darkness. Mireille's piercing voice follows me into oblivion.

Then nothing more....

Nothing more.

The cloud that blots out consciousness lifts for an instant—is it a moment later? or hours later? Or years later?... I have no idea.

I feel that I am being lifted ... carried along ... then flung down. I feel my head thrown far back, my hair dragged from my forehead.... The world is full of rushing horrors, of tearing, racking pain.... Then again nothingmore.

Fritz?... Is it then that I see him laughing as he looks at me? He is standing near a red curtain—he is speaking to some one, but his eyes are upon me and he laughs....

Once more unconsciousness like a black velvet tunnel engulfs me.

Out of the darkness comes Louise's voice calling me softly ... then louder ... then screaming my name. I open my eyes. She is bending over me. She lifts me up ... she wraps a shawl round my head, she drags me along ... drags me down the steps and out of the house and down a stony road that leads to the woods.

It is not day and it is not night; it is dawn perhaps.

Thirst and a deathly sickness are upon me.... I can go no farther. I lean my head against a tree, the rough bark of it wounds my forehead as I slip to the ground and fall on the damp leaves and moss.

I moan and cry.

"Hush! for the love of heaven! Hush!" … It is Louise's voice. "Hide, hide, lie down!"

And she drags me into a deep ditch overgrown with brambles. We hear horses gallop past and men's voices, full guttural voices that we know and dread. They ride on. They are gone. No—they stop.

They have found widow Duroc's two little boys hiding in the bushes…. Little César is shouldering a wooden gun and points it at them. In a moment three of the men are off their horses…. The children must be punished.

The children are punished.

… Then the men ride on. But the torture of those children has reminded me of Mireille. "Mireille—" I cry. "We must go back and fetch Mireille!"

"Hush! Mireille is here."

Mireille is here! She is not dead? Then who is dead?

"No one, no one is dead," says Louise, "we are all three here."

No—no—no! Somebody is dead. Somebody has been killed, I know it. I know it. Who is it? Is it I—is it Chérie who is dead? Louise's arms are about me, her tears fall on my face.

Then once again the velvet mist falls, and the world is blotted out.

We are on board a ship, dipping and rising on green-grey waters….

Many people are around us; derelicts like ourselves….

Soon the white cliffs of England shine and welcome us.

CHAPTER XII

CHÉRIE'S DIARY

November 2nd (*All Souls*).—It is strange, but even yet the feeling comes over me now and again that somebody was murdered on that night. And, strangest of all, I cannot free myself of the thought that it was I—I, who was killed, I, who am no more. I cannot describe the feeling. Doubtless it is folly. It is weakness and shock. It is what the good English doctor who has been called in to see us all—especially to try and cure Mireille—calls "psychic trauma." He says Mireille is suffering from psychic trauma; that means that her soul has been wounded. Sometimes I feel as if my soul had not only been wounded but that it had been killed—murdered while I was unconscious. I feel as if it were only a ghost, a spectre that resembles me and bears my name, but not the real Chérie, that wanders in this English garden, that speaks and smiles, kisses and comforts Louise, prays for Claude and for Florian.

Florian! Florian! Where are you? Are you dead, too? Is this sense of annihilation, of unreality in me but an omen, a warning of your real death? My brave young lover, blue-eyed and gay, have you gone from life? If I wander through all the world, if I journey to the ends of the earth, shall I never meet you again?

Oh God! I wish we were all safely dead, Louise and I and poor little Mireille; all lying silent and at peace, with closed eyes and quiet folded hands. I often think how good it would be if we could all three escape from life, as we escaped from the foe-haunted wood that night; if we could silently slip away, out of the long days and the dark nights; out of the hot summers and the dreary winters; out of feverish youth and desolate old age; out of hunger and thirst, out of exile and home-sickness, out of the past and out of the future, out of love and out of hate. Oh! to lie in peace under the waving trees of the little cemetery in Bomal, all with quiet heart and closed eyes. And by our side like a marble hero, Florian, Florian as I have known and loved him, Florian faithful and brave and true.

… But what of Claude? What would he do alone in the world, poor lame Claude, whose country is ravaged, whose home is devastated, whose wife fears him, whose child cannot speak to him … and whose sister, though she lives, has been murdered in her sleep?

November 15th.—Doctor Reynolds called today. Louise said she wanted him. Then when he came she would not see him. She locked herself in her room, and nobody could persuade her to come down.

So it was I who took Mireille into the drawing-room where Mrs. Whitaker and the doctor were waiting for us. They were talking rather excitedly when I knocked at the door—at least Mrs. Whitaker was—but when we entered she did not say a word.

She looked me up and down and I felt sorry that I had Louise's old black frock on instead of the new navy suit they had made for me a month ago. But I cannot fasten it, it is so tight round my throat and waist. That reminds me that when Mrs. Whitaker said the other day that she wished Doctor Reynolds to see me, I laughed and told her about my dresses being so tight, assuring her therefore that there could not be much wrong with me. She did not laugh, however; on the contrary, she stared at me very strangely and fixedly, and did not answer.

I don't know what is wrong in the house, but everybody seems silent and constrained and not so kind as they used to be. Eva has been sent away to stay with friends in Hastings, and George, who is at Aldershot, comes home for a day or so every now and then, but hardly ever speaks to us. He wanders about the roads near the house, or goes into the garden, the sad rainy garden, flicking the wet grasses and flowerless plants with his riding-stick. He often glances up at the window where I sit as if he would like to speak to us; but if I nod and smile at him he looks at me for an instant and then turns away. I have an idea that his mother objects to his talking with us much. He wanted Louise or me to read French with him, but after the first day his mother had a long talk with him and he did not come to our sitting-room again.

Perhaps they are tired of having us in the house. I am not surprised. We are doleful creatures, and we all have something the matter with us. I myself sometimes imagine I am going into consumption; I feel so strange and faint, I feel so sick when I eat, and I have the most terrible pains in my chest. Also I am anæmic, I know. But still I don't cough. So perhaps I am all right.

When we went into the drawing-room today the kindly old doctor felt Mireille's pulse and spoke to her, but all the time he was looking at me, and so was Mrs. Whitaker. He asked me several questions and when I told him what I felt, he coughed and said, "Hm…. Yes. Quite so." At last he glanced at Mrs. Whitaker, who at once got up and left the room with Mireille.

The doctor then beckoned to me and took my hand.

"My poor girl," he said, "have you anything to tell me?"

I was frightened. "What do you mean? Am I going to die? Am I very ill?"

He shook his head. "No. Why should you die? People don't die—" he commenced, and stopped.

"What about Mireille?" I asked, feeling terrified, I knew not why.

"Now we are speaking of you," he said, quite sternly.

Again he stopped as if expecting me to say something. I was bewildered. Perhaps the old man was a little strange in his head.

He coughed once more and his face flushed. Then he said: "I am an old man, my dear. I am a father—" He stopped again. "And I know all the sadness and wickednesses of the world. You may confide in me."

I said: "Thank you very much. I am sure I can."

There was another long silence. He seemed to be waiting. Then he got up and his face was a little hard. "Well," he said, "perhaps you prefer speaking to Mrs. Whitaker."

"Oh no!" I exclaimed. "Why—not at all."

Again he waited. Then he took his hat and gloves. "Well—as you like," he said abruptly. "I cannot compel you to speak. You must go your own way. I suppose you have your reasons." And he left the room.

I stood petrified with wonder. What did he mean about my going my own way? Why did he seem displeased with me? As I opened the door to go back to my room, I heard him in the hall speaking to Mrs. Whitaker.

"No," he was saying. "I feel sure I am not mistaken. But she would not approach the subject at all."

What a queer nightmare world we are living in!

Later.—I am expected to say something, I know not what. Everybody looks at me with an air of expectation—that is to say, Mrs. Whitaker does. But strangest thing of all, I sometimes think that Loulou does too. There are long silences between us, and when I raise my eyes I find her looking at me with a sort of breathless eagerness, an expression of anxiety and suspense of which I cannot grasp the meaning.

Late at night.—Mrs. Whitaker was very strange this evening. She came into my bedroom without warning, and found me on my knees. I was weeping and saying my prayers. She suddenly came towards me with an impulsive gesture of kindness and took me in her arms.

"Poor little girl!" she said, and she kissed me. She added, as if she were echoing the sentiments of the kind old doctor, "Chérie, I am a mother—" Then she stopped. "And I am not such a sour, hard person as I look." The tears stood in her eyes so I took her hand and kissed it. She sat down on a low chair and drew me to a footstool beside her. "Tell me," she said. "Tell me everything. I shall understand."

So I told her. I told her how unhappy I was about Louise and Mireille, I told her about Claude in the hospital. She said, "I know all that. Go on." Then I told her about Florian, how brave and handsome he was, and that we were betrothed. Then I wept bitterly and told her I thought that he was dead.

She raised my face with her hand and looked into my eyes. "Is it he?" she said.

I did not understand. She repeated her question. "Is it he? Did he—" she hesitated as if looking for a word—"did he wrong you?"

"Why? How wrong me?" I asked.

She gazed deeply into my eyes and I gazed back as steadfastly at her, wondering what she meant.

"Did he betray you?"

"Betray me? Never!" I cried. "He could never betray. He is true and faithful as a saint."

I was hurt that she should have asked such a question. Florian, who has never looked at or thought of any woman but me! Betray me!

"Well," she said rising to her feet suddenly—her expression of rather cold dignity again reminded me of the doctor. "If it had been the outrage of an enemy I know you would have told me. However, let it be as you wish. I will say only this: where I could have pitied disgrace, I cannot condone deceit."

And she left me.

Am I dreaming, or are people in this country incomprehensible and demented?

CHAPTER XIII

Louise looked her doom in the face with steady eyes. No more hope, no more doubt was possible. This was November. The third month had passed.

What she had dreaded more than death had come to pass. From the first hour the fear of it had haunted her. Now she knew. She knew that the outrage to which she had been subjected would endure; she knew that her shame would live.

In the middle of the night after tossing sleeplessly for hours, the full realization of this struck her heart like a blow. She sat up with clenched teeth in the darkness, her hands pressed to her temples.

After a while she slid from her bed and stood motionless in the middle of the room. Around her the world was asleep. She was alone with her despair and her horror.

How should she elude her fate? How should she flee from herself and the horror within her?

She turned on the light and went with quick steps to the mirror. There she stood with bare feet in her long white nightdress, staring at herself. Yes. She nodded and nodded like a demented creature at the reflection she saw before her. She recognized the aspect of it; the dragged features, the restless eyes, the face that seemed already too small for her body, the hunted anxious look. That was maternity. To violence nature had conceded what had been withheld from love. What she and Claude had longed for, had prayed for—another child— behold, now it was vouchsafed to her.

With teeth clenched she gazed at her white-draped reflection, she gazed at the hated fragile frame in which the eternal mystery of life was being accomplished. With the groan of a tortured animal she hid her face in her hands. What should she do? Oh God! what should she do?

Then began for Louise the heartbreaking pursuit of liberation, the nightmare, the obsession of deliverance.

All was vain. Nature pursued its inexorable course.

Then she determined that she must die. There was no help for it—she must die. She dreaded death; she was tied to life by a two-fold instinct—her own and that of the unborn being within her. How tenacious was its hold on life! It would not die and free her. It clung with all its tendrils to its own abhorred existence. Every night as she lay awake she pictured what it would be if it were born—this creature conceived in savagery and debauch, this child that she loathed and dreaded. She could imagine it living—a demon, a monster, a thing to shriek at, to make one's blood run cold. Waking and in her dreams she saw it; she saw it crawling like a reptile, she saw it stained with the colour of blood, she saw it babbling and mouthing at her, frenzied and insane.... That is what she would give life to, that is what she would have to nurse and to nourish; carrying that in her arms she would go to meet her husband when he came limping back from the war on his crutches.

She pictured that meeting with Claude in a hundred different ways, all horrible, all dreadful beyond words. Claude staring at her, not believing, not understanding.... Claude going mad.... Claude lifting his crutch and crushing the child's skull with it, as Amour's skull had been crushed—ah! the dead horrible Amour that she had seen when she staggered out of the room at dawn that day!... That was the first thing she had seen—that gruesome animal with its brains beaten out and its gleaming teeth uncovered. She could see it now, she could always see it when she closed her eyes! What if this sight had impressed itself so deeply upon her.... Hush! this was insanity; she knew that she was going mad.

So she must die.

How should she die? And when she was dead, what would happen to Mireille? And to Chérie?

Chérie! At the thought of Chérie a new rush of ideas overwhelmed Louise's wandering brain. Chérie! What was the matter with Chérie?

Had not she also that tense look, those pinched features, all those unmistakable signs that Louise well knew how to interpret? Was it possible that the same doom had overtaken her?

Then Louise forced herself to remember what she would have given her life to forget. With eyes closed, with shuddering soul, she compelled herself to live over again the darkest hours of her life.

... Before daybreak on the 5th of August. The house was silent. The invaders had gone. Louise, a livid spectre in the pale grey dawn, had staggered from her room—passing the dead Amour on Chérie's threshold—and had stumbled down the stairs. There at the foot of the wrought-iron banister lay Mireille, her mouth open, her breath coming in gasps, like a little dying bird.

Louise had raised her, had unwound the long scarf that bound her, had sprinkled water on her face and poured brandy down her throat ... until Mireille had opened her eyes. Then Louise had seen that they were not Mireille's eyes. There was frenzy and vacancy in the pale orbs that wandered round the room, wandered and wandered—until they stopped and were fixed, suddenly wild, hallucinated and intent. On what were they fixed with such an expression of unearthly terror? The mother turned to see.

Mireille's wild gaze was fixed upon a door, the red-curtained door of a bedroom. It was a spare room, seldom used; sometimes a guest or one of Claude's patients had slept there.

It was on this door—now flung wide open and with the red drapery torn down —that Mireille's wild, meaningless gaze was fixed. Louise looked. Then she looked again, without moving. She could see that the electric lights were burning in the room; a chair was overturned in the doorway, and there, there on the bed, lay a figure—Chérie! Chérie still in her white muslin dress all torn and bloodstained, Chérie with her two hands stretched upwards and tied to the bedpost above her head. A wide pink ribbon had been torn from her hair and used to tie her hands to the brass bedstead. Her face was scratched and bleeding. She was quite unconscious. Louise thought she was dead.

Ah! how had she found the strength to lift her, to call her, to drag her back to life, weeping over her and Mireille, gazing with maddened despair from one unconscious figure to the other?... She had dressed them, she had dragged and carried them down the stairs at the back of the house. Should she call for help? Should she go crying their shame and despair down the village street? No! no! Let no one see them. Let no one know what had befallen them....

And—listen! Was that not the clatter of Uhlans galloping down the road?

Moaning, staggering, stumbling, she dragged and carried her two helpless burdens into the woods....

There, the next evening a party of Belgian Guides had found them.

CHAPTER XIV

The Vicar of Maylands, the Reverend Ambrose Yule, was in his study writing his monthly contribution to the *Northern Ecclesiastical Review*. He was interested in his subject—"Our Sinful Sundays"—and his thoughts flowed smoothly on the topic of drink, frivolous talk and open kinematograph theatres. He wrote quickly and fluently in his neat small handwriting. A knock at the door interrupted him.

"Yes? What is it?" he asked somewhat impatiently.

"A lady to see you, sir," said Parrot, the comely maid.

"A lady? Who is it? I thought every one knew that I do not receive today."

"It is one of the foreign ladies staying with Mrs. Whitaker, sir."

"Oh, well. Show her into the drawing-room, and tell your mistress."

"I beg your pardon, sir, but——" a smile flickered over Parrot's mild face —"she asked specially for you. She said she wished to speak to 'Mr. the Clergyman' himself. First she said, 'Mr. the Cury' and then she said, 'Mr. the Clergyman.'"

"Well," sighed the vicar, "show her in." He placed a paper-weight on his neatly written sheets, rose and awaited his visitor standing on the hearthrug with his back to the fire.

Parrot ushered in a tall figure in black and then withdrew. The vicar stepped forward and found himself gazing into the depths of two resplendent dark eyes set in a very white face.

"Pray sit down," he said, "and tell me in what way I can be of service to you."

"May I speak French?" asked the lady in a low voice.

"*Mais certainement, Madame,*" said the courtly clergyman, who twenty or thirty years ago had studied Sinful Sundays abroad with intelligence and attention.

The lady sat down and was silent. She wore black cotton gloves and held in her hands a small handkerchief, which she clutched and crumpled nervously into a little ball.

The kindly vicar with his head on one side waited a little while and then spoke. "You are staying in Maylands? In Mrs. Whitaker's house, I believe? Have I not seen you, with two young girls?"

"Yes. My daughter and my sister-in-law." Louise's voice was so low that he had to bend forward to catch her words.

"Indeed. Yes." The vicar joined his finger-tips together, then disjoined them, then clapped them lightly together, waiting for further enlightenment. As it was not forthcoming he inquired: "May I know your name, Madame?"

"Louise Brandès."

"And ... er—monsieur your husband——?" the vicar's face was interrogative and prepared for sympathy.

"He is wounded, in hospital, at Dunkirk."

"Sad, sad," said the vicar, gently shaking his handsome grey head. "And ... you wish me to help you to go and see him?"

"No!" Louise uttered the word like a cry. Sudden tears welled up into her eyes, rolled rapidly down her cheeks and dropped upon her folded hands in their black cotton gloves.

"*Alors?* ..." interrogated the vicar, with his head still more on one side.

Louise raised her dark lashes and looked at the kind handsome face before her, looked at the narrow benevolent forehead, the firm straight lips, the beautiful hands (the vicar knew they were beautiful hands) with the finger- tips lightly pressed together. Instinctively she felt that here she would find no help. She knew that if she asked for pity, for protection, for money, it would be given her. But she also knew that what she was about to crave would meet with a stern repulse.

She had made up her mind that this was to be her last appeal for help, her last effort to obtain release. He was the priest, he was the representative of the All-Merciful....

She made the sign of the cross, she dropped on her knees and grasped his hand. "*Mon pere,*" she said—thus she used to address the Curé of Bomal, butchered on that never-to-be-forgotten night. "I will tell you——"

The vicar withdrew his hand from her grasp. "I beg you, madam, not to address me in that way. Also pray rise from your knees and take a seat." Ah me! how melodramatic were the Latin races! Poor woman! as if all this were necessary in order, probably, to ask for a few pounds, or to say that she could not get on with the peppery Mrs. Whitaker.

Louise had blushed crimson and risen quickly to her feet. "I am sorry," she said.

And then the kind vicar blushed too and felt that he had behaved like a brute.

At that moment the door opened and Mrs. Yule entered the room. With her was Dr. Reynolds, carrying a black leather bag.

"Oh!" exclaimed Mrs. Yule, catching sight of Louise. "I am sorry, Ambrose. I did not know you had a visitor."

"All right, dear," said the vicar; "this is Madame Brandès, who is staying with the Whitakers. She wants to consult me on some personal matter." Then he turned to Dr. Reynolds. "Well, doctor; how do you find our boy?"

"Quite all right. Quite all right," said the doctor. "We shall have him up and playing football again in no time. It is nothing but a strained tendon. Absolutely nothing at all."

Mrs. Yule had gone towards Louise with outstretched hand. "How do you do? I am glad to meet you," she said cordially. "You will stay for tea with us, I hope. My daughter, too, will be so pleased to see you. Not"—she added, with a little break in her voice—"that she really can see you. Perhaps you have heard that my dear daughter is blind."

"Blind!" Like a tidal wave the sorrow of the world seemed to overwhelm Louise. She felt that the sadness of life was too great to be borne. "Blind," she said. Then she covered her face and burst into tears.

Mrs. Yule's maternal heart melted; her maternal eyes noted the broken attitude, the tell-tale line of the figure! she stepped quickly forward, holding out both her hands.

"Come, my dear; sit down. Will you let me take your hat off? This English weather is so trying if one is not used to it," murmured Mrs. Yule with Anglo-Saxon shyness before the stranger's unexpected display of feeling, while the two men turned away and talked together near the window. Mrs. Yule pressed Louise's black-gloved hand in hers. What though this outburst were due, as it probably was, to the woman's condition, to her overwrought nerves, or to who knows what grief and misery of her own? The fact remained—and Mrs. Yule never forgot it—that this storm of tears was evoked by the news of her dear child's affliction. Mrs. Yule's heart was touched.

"You are Belgian, I know," she said in French, sitting down beside Louise and taking one of the black-gloved hands in her own. "I myself was at school in Brussels." And indeed her French was perfect, with just a little touch of Walloon closing the vowels in some of her words. "I would have called on you long ago—I would have asked you to make friends with my daughter whose affliction has so distressed your kind heart; but as you may have heard, my boy met with an accident, and I have not left the house for many days…. Do wait a moment, Dr. Reynolds," she added as the doctor approached to bid her good-bye. And turning to Louise she introduced him to her as "the kindest of friends and the best of doctors."

"We have met," said Dr. Reynolds, shaking hands with Louise and looking keenly into her face with his piercing, short-sighted eyes. "Madame Brandès's little daughter," he added, turning to Mrs. Yule, "is a patient of mine." There was a moment's silence; then the doctor, turning to the vicar, added in a lower voice: "It seems that their home was invaded, and the child terribly frightened. It is a very sad case. She has lost her reason and her power of speech."

Mrs. Yule in her turn was deeply moved and quick tears of sympathy gathered in her eyes. With an impulse of tenderest pity she bent suddenly forward and kissed the exile's pale cheek.

Like a flash of lightning in the night, it was revealed to Louise that now or never she must make her confession, now or never attempt a supreme, ultimate effort. This must be her last struggle for life. As she looked from Mrs. Yule's kind, tear-filled eyes to the calm, keen face of the physician hope bounded within her like a living thing. The blood rushed to her cheeks and she rose to her feet.

"Doctor!..." she gasped. Then she turned to Mrs. Yule again, it seemed almost easier to say what must be said, to a woman. "I want to say something.... I must speak...." And again turning to the doctor—"Do you understand me if I speak French?"

Doctor Reynolds looked rather like a timid schoolboy, notwithstanding his spectacles and his red beard, as he replied: "Oh ... *oui, Madame. Je comprong.*"

The vicar stepped forward. Looking from Louise to his wife and to the doctor he said: "Perhaps I had better leave you...."

But Louise quickly extended a trembling hand. "No! Please stay," she pleaded. "You are a priest. You are the doctor of the soul. And my soul is sick unto death."

The vicar took her extended hand. "I shall be honoured by your confidence," he said in courtly fashion, and seating himself beside her waited for her to speak.

Nor did he wait in vain. In eloquent passionate words, in the burning accents of her own language, the story of her martyrdom was revealed, her torn and outraged soul laid bare.

In that quiet room in the old-fashioned English vicarage the ghastly scenes of butchery and debauch were enacted again; the foul violence of the enemy, the treason, the drunkenness, the ribaldry of the men who with "mud and blood" on their feet, had trampled on these women's souls—all lived before the horrified listeners, and the martyrdom of the three helpless victims wrung their honest British hearts.

Louise had risen to her feet—a long black figure with a spectral face. She was Tragedy itself; she was the Spirit of Womanhood crushed and ruined by the war; she was the Grief of the World.

And now she flung herself at the doctor's feet, her arms outstretched, her eyes starting from their orbits, imploring him, in a paroxysm of agony and despair, to release and save her.

She fell face-downwards at his feet, shaken with spasmodic sobs, writhing and quaking as if in the throes of an epileptic fit. Mrs. Yule and the doctor raised her and placed her tenderly on the couch. Water and vinegar were brought, and wet cloths laid on her forehead.

There followed a prolonged silence.

"Unhappy woman!" murmured the vicar, aghast. "Her mind is quite unhinged."

"Yes," said the doctor; but he said it in a different tone, his experienced eye taking in every detail of the tense figure still thrilled and shaken at intervals by a convulsive tremor. "Yes, undoubtedly. She is on the verge of insanity." He paused. Then he looked the vicar full in the face. "And unless she is promptly assisted she will probably become hopelessly and incurably insane."

A low cry escaped Mrs. Yule's lips. "Oh, hush!" she said, bending over the pallid woman on the couch, fearful lest the appalling verdict might have reached her. But Louise's weary spirit had slipped away into unconsciousness.

"A sad case—a terribly sad case," said the vicar, thoughtfully pushing up his clipped grey moustache with his finger-tips and avoiding the doctor's resolute gaze. "She shall have our earnest prayers."

"And our very best assistance," said the doctor.

As if the words of comfort had reached her, Louise sighed and opened her eyes.

Mrs. Yule's protecting arm went round her.

"Of course, of course," said Mr. Yule to the doctor. Then he crossed the room and stood by the couch, looking down at Louise. "You will be brave, will you not? You must not give way to despair. We are all here to help and comfort you."

Louise raised herself on her elbow and looked up at him. A dazzling light of hope illuminated her face. Mr. Yule continued gravely and kindly.

"You can rely upon our friendship—nay, more—upon our tenderest affection. Our home is open to you if, as is most probable, Mrs. Whitaker desires you to leave her house. My wife and daughter will nurse and comfort you, will honour and respect you——" Louise broke into low sobs of gratitude as she grasped Mrs. Yule's hand and raised it to her lips. "And in the hour——" the vicar drew himself up to his full height and spoke in louder, more impressive tones—"and in the hour of your supreme ordeal, you shall not be forsaken."

Louise rose, vacillating, to her feet. "What … what do you mean?" she gasped. Her countenance was distorted; her eyes burned like black torches in her ashen face.

"I mean," declared the clergyman, his stern eyes fixed relentlessly, almost threateningly, upon the trembling woman, "I mean that whatever you may have suffered at the hands of the iniquitous, you have no right"—he raised his hand and his resonant voice shook with the vehemence of his feeling—"no right yourself to contemplate a crime."

A deep silence held the room. The sacerdotal authority wielded its powerful sway.

"A crime! a crime!" gasped Louise, and the convulsive tremor seized her anew. "Surely it is a greater crime to drive me to my death."

"The laws of nature are sacred," said the vicar, his brow flushing, a diagonal vein starting out upon it; "they may not be set aside. All you can do is humbly to submit to the Divine law."

Louise raised her wild white face and gazed at him helplessly, but Dr. Reynolds stepped forward and stood beside her. "My dear Yule," he said gravely, "do not let us talk about Divine law in connection with this unhappy woman's plight. We all know that every law, both human and Divine, has been violated and trampled upon by the foul fiends that this war has let loose."

The vicar turned upon him a face flushed with indignation. "Do you mean to say that this would justify an act which is nothing less than murder?"

The doctor made no reply and the vicar looked at him, aghast.

"Reynolds, my good friend! You do not mean to tell me that you would dare to intervene?"

Still the doctor was silent. Louise, her ashen lips parted, her wild eyes fixed upon the two men, awaited her sentence.

"I can come to no hasty decision," said the man of science at last. "But if on further thought I decide that it is my duty—as a man and a physician—to interrupt the course of events, I shall do so." He paused an instant while his eye studied the haggard face and trembling figure of Louise. "*A priori*," he added, "this woman's mental and physical condition would seem to justify me in fulfilling her wish."

"Ah!" It was a cry of delirious joy from Louise. She was tearing her dress from her throat, gasping, catching her breath, shaken with frenzied sobs in a renewed spasm of hysteria.

They had to lift her to the couch again. The doctor hurriedly dissolved two or three tablets of some sedative drug and forced the beverage through Louise's clenched teeth. Then he sat down beside her, holding her thin wrist in his fingers. Soon he felt the disordered intermittent pulse beat more rhythmically; he felt the tense muscles slacken, the quivering nerves relax.

Then he turned to the vicar, who stood with his back to the room looking out of the window at the dreary rain-swept garden.

"Yule," he said, "I shall be sorry if in following the dictates of my conscience I lose a life-long friendship—a friendship which has been very precious to me." The vicar neither answered nor moved; but Mrs. Yule came softly across the room and stood beside the doctor—the man who had healed and watched over her and those she loved, who fifteen years before had so tenderly laid her little blind daughter in her arms. She remained at his side with flushed cheeks, and her lips moved silently as if in prayer. Her husband stood motionless, looking out at the misty November twilight.

"Still more does it grieve me," continued the doctor, "to think that any act of mine should wound your feelings on a point of conscience which evidently touches you so deeply. But be that as it may, I must obey the dictates of common humanity which, in this case, coincide exactly with the teachings of science. Given the condition in which I find this woman, I feel that I must try my best to save her reason and her life. The chances are a hundred to one that if the child lived it would be abnormal; a degenerate, an epileptic." The doctor stepped near the couch and looked down at the unconscious Louise. "And as for the mother," he added, pointing to the pitiful death-like face, "look at her. Can you not see that she is well on her way to the graveyard or the madhouse?"

There was no reply. In the silence that followed Mrs. Yule drew near to her husband; but he kept his face resolutely turned away and stared out of the window.

She touched his arm tremulously. "Think, dear," she murmured, "think that she has a husband—whom she loves, who is fighting in the trenches for her and for his home. When he returns, will it not be terrible enough for her to tell him that his own daughter has lost her reason? Must she also go to meet him carrying the child of an enemy in her arms?"

The vicar did not answer. He turned his pale set face away without a word, and left the room.

CHAPTER XV

Dusk, the dreary November dusk, had fallen as Louise hurried homeward across the damp fields and deserted country roads. She had refused Mrs. Yule's urgent offer to accompany her or to send some one with her. She wanted to be alone—alone to look her happiness in the face, alone with her new heaven-sent ecstasy of gratitude. After the nightmare-days of hopelessness and despair, behold! life was to be renewed, retrieved, redeemed. Like a grey cloak of misery her anguish fell away from her; she stepped forth blissful and entranced into the pathway of her reflowering youth.

And with the certainty of this deliverance came the faith and hope in all other joys. Claude would return to her; Belgium would be liberated and redeemed. Mireille would find her speech again! Yes, Mireille would find her sweet, soft smile and her sweet shrill laughter. Might it not be Louise's own gloom that had plunged the sensitive soul of her child into darkness? Surely now that the storm-cloud was to be lifted from her, also the over-shadowed child-spirit would flutter back again into the golden springlight of its day. Surely all joys were possible in this most beautiful and joyous world. And Louise went with quick, light steps through the gloaming, half-expecting to see Mireille, already healed, come dancing towards her, gay and garrulous, calling her as she used to do by her pet name, "Loulou!"

Or it might be Chérie who would run to meet her, waving her hand to tell her that the miracle had come to pass!

Chérie! The name, the thought of Chérie struck at Louise's heart like a sudden blow. Her quick footsteps halted. As if a gust of the November wind had blown out the light of her happiness, she stood suddenly still in the middle of the road and felt that around her there was darkness again.

Chérie!... What was it that the doctor had said to her as he came with her to the gate of the Vicarage, as he held her hand in his firm, strong grasp, promising to save her from the deep waters of despair? What were the words she had then neither understood nor answered, borne away as she was on the wave of her own tumultuous joy? They suddenly came back to her now; they suddenly reached her hearing and comprehension. He had said, looking her full in the face with a meaning gaze, "What about your sister?"

"What about your sister?" Your sister. Of course he had meant Chérie. What about her? What about her? Again Louise felt that dull thud in her heart as if some one had struck it, for she knew, she knew what he meant—she knew what there was about Chérie.

There was the same abomination, the same impending horror and disgrace. Had not Chérie herself come and told her, in bewilderment and simplicity, of the strange questionings, the obscure warnings Mrs. Whitaker and the doctor had subjected her to? Ah, Louise knew but too well what it all meant; Louise knew but too well what there was about Chérie that even to strangers was manifest and unmistakable. Yes, Louise had dreaded it, had felt it, had known it—though Chérie herself had not. But until now her own torment of body and soul had hidden all else from her gaze, had made all that was not her own misery as unreal and unimportant as a dream. Vaguely, in the background of her thoughts, she had known that there was still another disaster to face, another fiery ordeal to encounter, but swept along in the vortex of her own doom she had flung those thoughts aside; in her own life-and-death struggle she had not stopped to ask, What of that other soul driving to shipwreck beside her, broken and submerged by the self-same storm?

But now it must be faced. She must tell the unwitting Chérie what the future held for her. She must stun her with the revelation of her shame.

For Louise understood—however incredible it might seem to others—that Chérie was wholly unaware of what had befallen her on that night when terror, inebriety, and violence had plunged her into unconsciousness. Not a glimmer of the truth had dawned on her simplicity, not a breath of knowledge had touched her inexperience. Sullied and yet immaculate, violated and yet undefiled—of her could it indeed be said that she had conceived without sin.

Louise went on in the falling darkness with lagging footsteps. Deep down in her heart her happiness hid its face for the sorrow and shame she must bring to another.

Then she remembered—with what deep thankfulness!—that though she must inflict this hideous hurt on Chérie, yet she could also speak to her of help, she could promise her release and the hope of ultimate peace and oblivion.

She hurried forward through the darkening lanes, and soon joy awoke again and sang within her. Yes! There they stood at the open gate, the two beloved waiting figures—the taller, Chérie, with her arm round the slender form of Mireille. Louise ran towards them with buoyant step.

"Louise!" cried Chérie. "Where have you been? How quickly you walk! How bright and happy you look! Why, I could see your smile shining from far off in the darkness!"

Louise kissed the soft, cold cheeks of both; she took Chérie's warm hand and the chilly little hand of Mireille and went with them towards the house. How cheerful were the lighted windows seen through the trees! How sheltered and peaceful was this refuge! How gracious and generous were the strangers who had housed and nourished them!

How kind and good and beautiful was life!

***

"Tell me the truth, Louise," said Chérie that evening, when, having seen little Mireille safely asleep, Louise returned to the cheerful sitting-room, where the dancing firelight gleamed on the pink walls and cosy drawn curtains. "Tell me the truth. You have heard something—something from Claude ... something ——" Chérie flushed to the lovely low line of the growth of her auburn curls —"from Florian! You have, you have! I can read it in your face. You have had news of some kind."

Yes—Louise had had news.

"Good news——"

Yes. Good news. She sat down on a low armchair near the fire and beckoned with her finger. "Chérie!"

The girl came quickly to her side and sat down on the rug at her feet. The fire danced and flickered on her red-gold hair and milkwhite oval face.

"Chérie." ... Louise's voice was low, her eyes cast down. She felt like a torturer, she felt as if she were murdering a flower, tearing asunder the closed petals of this girlish soul and filling its cup with poison.

Chérie was looking up into her face with a radiant, expectant smile.

How should she tell her? How should she tell her?...

Louise bent forward and covered the shining, questioning eyes with her hand. "Tomorrow, Chérie! Tomorrow."

***

CHAPTER XVI

On the morrow Chérie awoke early. She could not say what had startled her out of a deep restful slumber, but suddenly she was wide awake, every nerve tense in a kind of strained expectancy, waiting she knew not for what. Something had occurred, something had awakened her; and she was waiting for it to repeat itself; waiting to hear or feel it again. But whatever it was, sound or sensation, it was not repeated.

Chérie rose quickly, slid her feet into her slippers, and went across the room to the window. She leaned out with her bare elbows on the window-sill and looked at the garden—at the glistening lawn, at the stripped trees, dark and clear-cut against the early sky. It was a rose-grey dawn, as softly luminous as if it were the month of February instead of November. There seemed to be a promise of spring in the pale radiance of the morning.

She knew she could not sleep any more; so she dressed quietly and quickly, wrapped a scarf round her slim shoulders, and went down into the garden.

George Whitaker also had awakened early. These were his last few days at home before leaving for the front, and his spirit was full of feverish restlessness. His sister Eva was expected back from Hastings that morning and they would spend two or three happy days together before he left for the wonderful, and awful adventure of war. He had obeyed his mother's desire, and had not seen or spoken to their Belgian guests for many days. Indeed, it was easy—too easy, thought George with a sigh—to avoid them, for they seemed day by day to grow more shy of strangers and of friends. George only caught fleeting glimpses of them as they passed their windows; sometimes he saw a gleam of auburn hair where Chérie sat with bent head near the schoolroom balcony, reading or at work.

This morning, as he stood vigorously plying his brushes on his bright hair and gazing absent-mindedly at the garden, he caught sight of Chérie, with a scarf round her shoulders and a book in her hand, walking down the gravel pathway towards the summer-house. He flung down his brushes, finished dressing very quickly, and ran downstairs. After all, he was leaving in forty- eight hours or so—leaving to go who knows where, to return who knows when. He might never have such another chance of seeing her and saying good-bye. True, it was rather soon to say good-bye. He would probably be meeting her every moment during the next two days. Eva was coming back, and would be sure to want her little foreign friend always beside her. Eva had a way of slipping her arm through Chérie's and drawing her along, saying:

"Allons, Chérie!" which was very pleasant in George's recollection. He also would have liked to slip his arm through the slim white arm of the girl and say, *"Allons, Chérie!"* He could imagine the flush, or the frown, or the fleeting marvel of her smile....

In a few moments he was downstairs, out of the house, and running towards the summer-house. But she was not there.

He found her walking slowly beside the little artificial lake in the shrubbery, reading her book.

"Good-morning," he said in tones exaggerately casual, as she looked up in surprise.

"Good-morning, Monsieur George," she said, and the softness of the "g's" in her French accent was sweet to his ear.

"What are you doing, up so early?"

"Et vous?" she retorted, with her brief vivid smile.

"I ... I ... have come to say good-bye," he said.

"Good-bye? Why, I thought you were not going away until the day after tomorrow."

"Right-o," said George. "No more I am. But you know what a time I take over things; the mater always calls me a slow-coach. I—I like beginning to pack up and say good-bye days and weeks before it is time to go." Again he watched the little half-moon smile that turned up the corners of her mouth and dimpled her rounded cheek.

"Well then—good-bye," she said, looking up at him for an instant and realizing that she would be sorry when he had left.

"Good-bye." He took her book from her and held out his hand. She placed her own soft small hand in his, and he found not another word to say. So he said "Good-bye" again, and she repeated it softly.

"But now you must go away," she said. "You cannot keep on saying good-bye and staying here."

"Of course not," said George. "I'll go in a minute." Then he cleared his throat. "I wonder if you will be here when I come back. I suppose you would hate to live in England altogether, wouldn't you?"

"I don't know. I have never thought of it," said Chérie.

"Well—but do you like England? Or don't you?"

"S'il vous plaît Londres?" quoted Chérie, glancing up at him and laughing.

Surely, thought George, no other eyelashes in the world gave such a starry look to two such sea-blue eyes.

"In some ways I do not like England," she remarked, thoughtfully. "I do not like—I mean I do not understand the English women. They seem so—how shall I say?—so hard … so arid…." She plucked a little branch from a bush of winter-berries and toyed with it absently as she walked beside him. "They all seem afraid of appearing too friendly or too kind."

"Perhaps so," said George.

"When we first came here your sister warned me about it. She said, 'You must never show an English woman that you like her; it is not customary, and would be misunderstood.'"

"That's so. We don't approve of gush," said George.

"If you call nice things by horrid names they become horrid things," said Chérie sternly and sententiously. "Natural impulses of friendliness are not 'gush.' When I first meet strangers I always feel that I like them; and I go on liking them until I find out that they are not nice."

"You go the wrong way round," said George. "In England we always dislike people until we know they are all right. Besides, if you were to start by being sweet and amiable to strangers, they would probably think you wanted to borrow money from them, or ask them favours."

"How mean-minded!" exclaimed Chérie.

George laughed. "You should see the mater," he said, "how villainously rude she is to people she meets for the first time. That is what makes her such a social success."

Chérie looked bewildered. George was silent a moment; then he spoke again.

"And what do you think about the English men? Do you dislike them too?"

"I don't really know them," said Chérie; "but they—they *look* very nice," and she turned her blue eyes full upon him, taking a quick survey of his handsome figure and fair, frank face.

George felt himself blush, and hated himself for it.

"You—you would never think of marrying an Englishman, would you?"

Chérie shook her head, and the long lashes drooped over the sea-blue stars. "I am affianced to be married," she said with her pretty foreign accent, "to a soldier of Belgium."

"Oh, I see," said George rather huskily and hurriedly. "Of course. Quite so."

They walked along in silence for a little while. Then he opened her book, which he still held in his hand. "What were you reading? Poetry?"

He glanced at the fly-leaf, on which were written the words "*Florian Audet, à Chérie,*" and he quickly turned the page. "Poetry" ... he said again, "by Victor Hugo." Then he added, "Why, this sounds as if it were written for you: '*Elle était pâle et pourtant rose....*' That is just what you are."

Chérie did not answer. What was this strange flutter at her heart again? It frightened her. Could it be angina pectoris, or some other strange and terrible disease? Not that it hurt her; but it thrilled her from head to foot.

"You are quite *pâle et pourtant rose* at this very moment," repeated George, looking at her. Then he added rather bitterly as he handed her back the book, "I suppose you are thinking of the day when you will marry your soldier-lover."

"Perhaps I shall not live to marry anybody," said Chérie in a low voice.

"What an idea!" exclaimed George.

"And as for him," she continued, "he will probably be killed long before that."

"Oh no," said George, "I'm sure he won't. And I'm sure you will.... And I'm sure you're both going to be awfully happy. As for me," he added quickly, "I am going to have no end of a good time. I believe I am to be sent to the Dardanelles. Doesn't the word sound jolly! 'The Dardanelles!' It has a ring and a lilt to it...." He laughed and pushed his hair back from his clear young forehead.

"Good luck to you," said Chérie, looking up at him with a sudden feeling of kindness and regret.

They had turned back, and were now passing the summer-house in full view of the windows of the house. On the schoolroom balcony they saw Louise. She beckoned, and Chérie hurried forward and stood under the balcony, looking up at her.

"Oh, Chérie! I wondered where you were," said Louise, bending over the ledge. "I was anxious. Come up, dear! I want to speak to you."

"Oh yes!" exclaimed Chérie eagerly, remembering Louise's promise of the night before. Then she turned to George. "I must go. So now we must really say good-bye." She laughed. "Or shall we say *au revoir?*"

"Let us say *au revoir,*" said George, looking her full in the face.

"*Au revoir*, Monsieur George! *Au revoir!*"

Then she went indoors.

Two days later George Whitaker went away.

They sent him to the Dardanelles.

And in this world there was never an *au revoir* for Monsieur George.

CHAPTER XVII

Louise stood in the doorway waiting for Chérie, and watched her coming up the stairs rather slowly with fluttering breath. She drew her into the room and shut the door.

Mireille sat quietly in her usual armchair by the window, with her small face lifted to the sky.

"Chérie," said Louise, drawing the girl down beside her on the wide old divan on which the little Whitakers had sprawled to learn their lessons in years gone by. "I have something to say to you."

"I knew you had," exclaimed Chérie, flushing. "I knew it yesterday when I saw you. It is good news!"

Louise hesitated. "Yes ... for me," she said falteringly, "it is good news. For you, my dear little sister, for you ... unless you realize what has befallen us—it may be very terrible news."

Chérie looked at her with startled eyes. "What do you mean?" she asked under her breath.

Louise put her hand to her neck as if something were choking her. Her throat was dry; she could find neither words nor voice in which to give to the waiting girl her message of two-fold shame.

"Chérie ... my darling ... I must speak to you about that night ... your birthday-night——"

Chérie started back. "No!" she cried. "You said when we came here that we were to forget it—that it was a dream! Why—why should you speak of it again?"

"Chérie," said Louise in a low voice, "perhaps for you." ... She faltered, "for you it may have been a dream. But not for me."

The girl sat straight upright, tense and alert. "What do you mean, Louise?"

"I mean that for me that night has borne its evil fruit. Chérie! I thought of killing myself. But yesterday ... I spoke to Dr. Reynolds. He has promised to save me."

"To save you!" gasped Chérie. "Louise! Louise! Are you so ill?"

"My darling, my own dear child, I am worse than ill. But there is help for me; I shall be saved—saved from dishonour and despair." She lowered her voice.

"Chérie!"—her voice fell so low that it could hardly be heard by the trembling girl beside her—"can you not understand? The shame I am called upon to face—the doom that awaits me—is maternity."

Maternity! Slowly, as if an unseen force uplifted her, Chérie had risen to her feet. Maternity!… The veil of the mystery was rent, the wonder was revealed! Maternity! That was the key to all her own strange and marvellous sensations, to the throb and the thrill within her! Maternity.

She stood motionless, amazed. A shaft of sunlight from the open window beat upon her, turning her hair to gold and her wide eyes to pools of wondering light. Such wonder and such light were about her that Louise gazed in awed silence at the ethereal figure, standing with pale hands extended and virginal face upturned.

She seemed to be listening…. To what voice? What annunciation did she harken to with those rapt eyes?

Louise called her by her name. But Chérie did not answer. Her lips were mute, her eyes were distant and unseeing. She heard no other voice but a child-voice asking from her the gift of life.

And to that voice her trembling spirit answered.

CHAPTER XVIII

Dr. Reynolds kept his promise to Louise.

In a private nursing-home in London the deed of mercy and of ruthlessness was accomplished. The pitiable spark of life was quenched.

Out of the depths of darkness and despair Louise, after wavering for many days on the threshold of death, came slowly back to life once more.

During the many weeks she was in the nursing-home she saw neither Chérie nor Mireille; but Mrs. Yule came nearly every day and brought good news of them both, saying how happy she and her husband were to have them at the Vicarage.

For Mr. Yule himself had gone to the Whitakers' house, an hour after Louise had left it with Dr. Reynolds, and had taken the two forlorn young creatures away. Their stricken youth found shelter in his house, where Mireille's affliction and Chérie's tragic condition were alike sacred to his generous heart.

The little blind girl, Lilian, adored them both. She used to sit between them—often resting her face against Mireille's arm, or holding the child's hand in hers—listening to Chérie's tales of their childhood in Belgium. She was never tired of hearing about Chérie's school-days at Mademoiselle Thibaut's *pensionnat*; of her trips to Brussels and Antwerp, and the horrors of the dungeons of Château Steen; of her bicycle-lessons on the sands of Westende under the instruction of the monkey-man; and above all of her visits to Braine l'Alleude and the battle-field of Waterloo, where she had actually drunk coffee in Wellington's sitting-room, and rested in his very own armchair....

Lilian, with her closed eyes and intent face—always turned slightly upward as if yearning towards the light—listened eagerly, exclaiming every now and then with a little excited laugh, "I see ... I see...." And those words and the sweet expression of the small ecstatic face made Chérie's voice falter and the tears suffuse her eyes.

One day a letter came. It was from Claude. He had almost completely recovered from his wound and was leaving the hospital in Dunkirk to go to the front again. He sent all his love and all God's blessings to Louise and to his little Mireille and to Chérie. They would meet again in the happier days soon to come. Had they news of Florian? The last he had heard of him was a card from the trenches at Loos....

And that same day—a snowy day in December—Louise at length returned from her ordeal and stood, a pale and ghostly figure, at the Vicarage door. To her also it opened wide, and her faltering footsteps were led with love and tenderness to the firelight of the hospitable hearth.

There in the vicar's leather armchair, with the vicar's favourite collie curled at her feet, sat Mireille; her soft hair parted in the middle and tied with a blue ribbon by Mrs. Yule; a gold bangle, given her by Lilian, on her slim wrist. With a cry of joy and gratitude Louise knelt before her, kissing the soft chill hands, the silent mouth, the eyes that did not recognize her.

"Mireille, Mireille! Can you not say a word to me? Not a word? Say, 'Welcome, mother!' Say it, darling! Say, '*Maman, bonjour.*'"

But the child's lips remained closed; the singing fountain of her voice was sealed.

The door opened, and Chérie entered the room—a Chérie altered and strange in her new and tragic dignity.

Louise involuntarily drew back, gazing in amazement at the significant change of form and feature; then with a sob of passionate pity she went to her and folded her in her arms.

Chérie, with a smile and a sigh, bowed her head upon Louise's breast.

CHAPTER XIX

To see Christmas in an English vicarage is to see Christmas indeed; and the love and charity and beauty of it sank deeply into the exiles' wounded hearts.

But one day came the summons to return to Belgium. It was a peremptory order from the German Governor of Brussels to all owners of house or property to return to their country with the least possible delay. The penalty of disregarding this summons would be the confiscation of all and any property owned by them in Belgium.

Louise stood in Chérie's room with the open letter in her hand, aghast and trembling.

"To return to Belgium? They ask us to return to Belgium?" Louise could scarcely pronounce the words. "Do you realize what it means, Chérie?"

"It means—going home," whispered the girl, with downcast eyes and a delicate flush mounting to her pale cheeks.

"Home! Do you remember what that home was when we left it?" cried Louise, her eyes blazing at the recollection.

"No," said Chérie, "I do not remember."

"Home! Home without Claude—without Florian! with half our friends killed or lost ..." cried Louise, and the easy tears of weakness flowed down her thin cheeks. "Home—with Mireille a silent ghost, and you—and you—" Her dark passionate eyes lit for an instant on the figure of her sister-in-law, and horror and shame seemed to grip at her throat. "Let us never speak of it again."

And she flung the paper into the fire.

But the memory of it she could not fling away. The possibility of returning to Belgium, which before had seemed so remote, the idea of seeing their home again which they had deemed lost to them for ever, now filled her mind and Chérie's to the exclusion of every other thought. That harsh call to return rang in their hearts by day and by night, awakening home-sickness and desire.

At night Louise would dream a thousand times of that return, a thousand times putting the idea from her with indignation and with fear. Every night she would imagine herself arriving at Bomal, hurrying through the village streets to the gate of her house, entering it, going up the stairs, opening the door to Claude's study....

Little by little home-sickness wound itself like a serpent about her heart, crushing her in its strong spirals, poisoning with its virulent fang every hour of her day. Little by little the nostalgic yearning, the unutterable longing to hear her own language, to be among her own people—though tortured, though oppressed, though crushed by the invader's heel—grew in her heart until she felt that she could bear it no longer. The sense of exile became intolerable; the sound of English voices, the sight of English faces, hurt and oppressed her; the thought of the wild English waters separating her from her woeful land seemed to freeze and drown her heart.

A week after she had told Chérie never to speak about it any more she thought of nothing else, she dreamed of nothing else, but to return to her home, her wrecked and devastated home, there to await Claude in hope, in patience, and in prayer.

She would feel nearer to him when once the icy, tumbling waves of the Channel separated them no more. She would be ready for him when the day of deliverance came, the day of Belgium's freedom and redemption—surely, surely now it could not be far off! Claude would find her there, in her place, waiting for him. She would see him from afar off, she would be at the door to meet him as she always was when he had gone away even for a few days or hours. His little Mireille, alas! was stricken, but might she not before then recover? His sister—ah! His sister!... Louise wrung her hands and wept.

Late one night she went to Chérie's room. She opened the door very gently so as not to wake her if she were asleep. But Chérie was sitting near the fire bending over some needlework and singing softly to herself. She jumped up, blushing deeply, as Louise entered, and she attempted to hide her work in her lap. It was an infant's white cape she was embroidering, and as Louise saw it her own pale cheeks flushed too.

"Chérie," she faltered, "I have been thinking ... what if we went home?"

"Yes," said Chérie quietly, with the chastened calmness of those whose mission it is to wait.

"Let us go, let us go," said Louise. "We will make our house ready and beautiful for those who will return."

"Yes," said Chérie, again.

"They will return and find us there ... waiting for them ... even though the storm has passed over us...." Her voice broke in a sob. "Mireille will recover, I know it, I feel it! And you—oh, Chérie!"—she dropped on her knees before the trembling girl—"you, you will be brave," she cried passionately, "before it is too late ... Chérie, Chérie, I implore you...."

Chérie was silent. It was as if she did not hear. It was as if she did not understand.

In vain Louise spoke of the shame of the past, of the woe and misery of the future. To all her wild words, to her caresses and entreaties, Chérie gave no reply. Her lips seemed mute, her eyes seemed distant and unseeing as those of the mindless, wandering Mireille.

At last she rose, and stood facing Louise, her face grave, inexorable, unflinching.

"Louise, say no more. No human reasoning, no human law, no human sanction or prohibition can influence me. No one may judge between a woman and the depths of her own body and soul; in so grave a matter each must decide according to her own conscience. What to the one is shame, hatred, and horror, to the other is joy, wonder, and love. To me, Louise, this suffering—tragic and terrible though it be—is joy, wonder, and love. I do not explain it, I do not justify it; I do not think I even understand it. But this I feel, that I would sooner tear out my living heart than voluntarily destroy the life which is within me, and which I feel is part of my very soul."

Louise was silent. She felt herself face to face with the great primeval instinct of maternity; and words failed her. Then the thought of their return to Belgium clutched at her heart again.

"But if we go home! Think, think of the shame of it! What will they say, those who have known us? Think—what will they say?"

Chérie sighed. "I cannot help what they say."

"And when Claude returns, Chérie! When Claude returns...."

Chérie bowed her head and did not answer.

Louise moved nearer to her. "And have you forgotten Florian? Florian, who loves you, and hoped to make you his wife?..."

The tears welled up into Chérie's eyes, but she was silent.

Louise's voice rose to a bitter cry. "Chérie! Think of the brutal hands that bound you, of the infamous enemy that outraged you. Think, think that you, a Belgian, will be the mother of a German child!"

But Chérie cared nothing, remembered nothing, heard nothing. She heard no other voice but that child-voice asking from her the gift of life, telling her that in the land of the unborn there are no Germans and no Belgians, no victors and no vanquished, but only the innocent flowers of futurity—the white- winged doves of Jesus, and the snowy lambs of God.

BOOK III

CHAPTER XX

Feldwebel Karl Sigismund Schwarz lay on the internal slope of a crater under a red sunset sky. His eyes were shut. But he was not asleep. He was making up his mind that he must move his left arm. Something heavy seemed to be pressing it down, crushing and crunching it. He would move it, he would lift it up in the air and feel the circulation return to it and the breezes of heaven blow on it. Never was there such a hot and heavy arm.... Yes. He would certainly lift it in a moment.

After this great mental exertion, Feldwebel Schwarz went to sleep for a few moments; then he woke up again, more than ever determined to move his arm. What did one do when one wanted to move one's arm? And where was his arm? Where was everything? Where was he, Karl Sigismund Schwarz?... There was evidently a 'cello playing somewhere quite close to him; he could hear it right in his head: "Zoom ... zoom-zoom ... zoom-zoom."

He said to himself that he knew where he was. He was in Charlottenburg, in the Café des Westens, and the Hungarian, Makowsky, was playing on the *Bassgeige*. Zoom ... zoom-zoom.... The rest of the orchestra would join in presently. Meanwhile, what was the matter with his arm? He groaned aloud and tried to raise himself on his right elbow. He could not do so; but in turning his head he caught sight of a man lying close beside him, a man in Belgian uniform lying flat on the ground with his profile turned to the sky. This convinced Schwarz that he was not in Charlottenburg after all. He was somewhere in Flanders near a rotten old city called Ypres; and he was lying in a hole made by a shell. He glanced sideways at the Belgian again. Then he cried out loud, "See here, what is the matter with my arm?" But the man did not answer, and Schwarz realized that he probably did not understand German. Probably, also, he was dead.

So Karl Schwarz lay back again, and listened to the 'cello buzzing in his brain.

The red sunset had faded into a drab twilight when in his turn the Belgian opened his eyes, sighed and sat up. He saw the wounded German lying beside him with limp legs outstretched, a mangled arm and a face caked with blood. The man's eyes were open, so the Belgian nodded to him and said, "*Ca va, mon vieux?*"

"*Verfluchter Schweinehund,*" replied Karl Schwarz; and Florian Audet, who did not understand that he was being called a damned swine-hound, nodded back again in a friendly way. Then each was silent with his thoughts.

Florian tried to realize what had happened. He tentatively moved one arm; then the other; then his feet and legs. He moved his shoulders a little; they seemed all right. He felt nothing but a pain in the back of his neck, like a violent cramp; otherwise there seemed nothing much the matter with him. Why was he lying there? Let him remember. There had been an order to attack … a dash over the white Ypres road and across the fields to the south … then an explosion—yes. That was it. He had been blown up. This was shock or something. He wondered where the remains of his company was and how things had turned out. There were sounds of firing not far away, the spluttering of rifles and the booming of the gun.

He tried to rise to his feet, but it was as if the earth rose with him. He could not get his hands off the ground—earth and sky whirled round him, and he had to lie down again.

Soon darkness came up out of the thundering east and blew out the twilight.

Meanwhile Feldwebel Schwarz was again in the Café des Westens; the orchestra of ten thousand *Bassgeigen* was booming like mad, and he was beating on the table with his heavy arm, calling for the waiter Max to bring him something cold to drink. Max came hurrying up and stood before him carrying a tray laden with glasses—huge cool Schoppen of Münchner and Lager, and tall glasses of lemonade with ice clinking in it. Which would he have? He could not make up his mind which he would have. His throat burned him, his stomach was on fire with thirst, and he could not say which of the cool drinks he wanted. He felt that he must drink them all—the iced Münchner, the chilly Lager, the biting lemonade—he must drink them all together, or die. Suddenly he noticed that the *Wasserleiche*—you know the *Wasserleiche*, the "Water-corpse" of the Café des Westens—the cadaverous- looking woman whose face is of such a peculiar hue that you would vow she had been drowned and left lying in the water for a couple of days before they fished her out again—well, she had come up to the waiter and was embracing him, and all the glasses were slipping off his tray. Ping!—pang!—down they crashed! Ping!—pang! smashing and crashing all around. You never heard glasses make such a noise. There was nothing left to drink—nothing in the wide world.

Then Feldwebel Schwarz began to cry. He heard himself moaning and crying, until Max the waiter looked at him and then he saw that it was not Max the waiter at all that the Water-corpse was embracing. She never did embrace men. It was her friend Mélanie, who stood there laughing with her mouth wide open, showing the pink roof of her mouth and her tiny wolfish teeth— the two eye-teeth slightly longer than the others and very pointed.

Karl Schwarz knew that if he wanted anything to drink he must be amiable to

Mélanie. He would sing her the song about "Gräfin Mélanie," beginning "*Nur für Natur....*"

But he could not remember it. He could only remember the Ueberbrettel song —

"Die Flundern
"Werden sich wundern...."

He sang this a great many times, and the waiter Max, who was lying on the floor among the broken glasses, applauded loudly. You never heard such clapping; it went right through one's head. But Mélanie did not give him anything to drink, and the Water-corpse—he suddenly remembered that she never allowed any one to speak to Mélanie—turned on him furiously and bit him in the arm. He howled with pain, and then Mélanie bent forward showing all her wolfish teeth, and she also bit him in the arm. They were tearing and mangling him. He could not get his arm away from the two dreadful creatures. "*Verdammte Sauweiber!*" he shouted at them, and his voice was so loud that it woke him.

He saw the star-strewn sky above him, and beside him the prostrate figure of the Belgian as he had seen him before. Probably, he said to himself, Mélanie and the Water-corpse had been at this man too. To keep them away he had to go on singing with his parched throat—

"Die Flundern
"Werden sich wundern...."
        *   *   *   *
"Die Flundern
"Werden sich wundern...."

He imagined that these words possessed some occult power which must keep the two horrible women away from him.

So he continued to repeat them all night long.

Between two and three o'clock Florian Audet opened his eyes and turned his head to look round. The wounded German's voice had roused him from sleep —or from unconsciousness—and he lay there vaguely wondering what that continually repeated cry might mean.

"*Die Flundern werden sich wundern....*" The words sank into his brain and remained there. Perhaps, he mused, it was some kind of national war-cry, a shout of victory or defiance ... "Death or liberty!..." or "In the name of the Kaiser," or something like that.

From where he was he could see the outstretched figure lying to the left of him, the limp legs, the helpless, upturned feet in their thick muddy boots; and he heard the sound of the rattling breath still repeating brokenly, "*Die Flundern werden sich wundern....*"

An overwhelming sense of pity came over him; pity for the broken figure beside him, pity for himself, pity for the world. With an immense effort, for he felt as if every bone were broken, he turned on his side and, struggling slowly along the ground, dragged himself towards the dying man. When he reached him and could touch him with his outstretched hand he rested awhile; then he fumbled for his brandy-flask, found it, unscrewed it and held it near the man's face.

"*Tiens! bois,*" he said. But the German did not move to take it; and soon the rattling breath stopped.

Florian wriggled a little closer, slipped his right arm under the man's head and raised it. Then by the grey April starlight he saw something bubble and gush over the man's face from a wound in his forehead. The German opened his eyes. What were those fiendish women doing to him now? Pouring warm wine over his head.... Through the tepid scarlet veil his wild eyes blinked up at Florian in childish terror and bewilderment. A wave of sickening faintness overcame Florian; his arm slackened, and his enemy's ghastly crimson face fell back upon it as Florian himself sank beside him in a swoon.

There they lay all through the night, side by side, like brothers, the living and the dead; the German soldier with his head on the Belgian officer's arm. And thus two German Red Cross men found them in the chilly dawn as they slid down the crater-side, carrying a folded stretcher between them. They were very young, the two Red Cross men; they had not finished studying philosophy in the Bonn University when the war had broken out, and they had left Kant and Hebel for a quick course of surgery. The youngest one, who had very fair hair, wrote foolish Latin poems, said to be after the style of Lucretius.

They dropped the stretcher and stood silently looking down at those two motionless figures in their fraternal embrace, whose attitude told their tale. Florian's hand, holding the open brandy-flask, lay on the dead German's breast; the ghastly dead face of their comrade was pillowed easily on the enemy's encircling arm.

Something rose in the throat of the two who gazed, and the younger one—the one who wrote Latin verse—bent down and laid his hand lightly, as if invoking a blessing on Florian's pale forehead. Then he turned with a start to his companion. "He is alive!"

The other in his turn touched the man's brow, then lifted the limp hand to feel his pulse. They knelt beside him and poured brandy down his throat. Then they worked over him for a long while, until a breath of life fluttered through the ashen lips, and the vague blue eyes opened and looked into theirs.

The Germans rose to their feet. The Belgian, when he had lain unconscious with his arm around their fallen comrade, had been to them a hero and a friend. Now, alive, with open eyes, he was their foe and their prisoner.

They spoke to him at first, not unkindly, in German; then, somewhat brusquely, in French; but he gave them no reply. His brain was benumbed and stupefied. He could not speak and he could not stand. So they lifted him and placed him on the stretcher.

"Poor devil!" murmured the younger man as he extended the two limp arms along the recumbent body and pointed out to his companion the right sleeve of the Belgian uniform sodden and stiff with the German soldier's blood.

"Poor devil! What have we saved him for? To send him to the hell of Wittemberg!…"

"Hard lines," murmured the other one.

"*Gerechter Gott!*" exclaimed the foolish fair-haired poet, "I wish we could give him a chance."

———————

They gave him a chance.

Florian never knew how it was that he found himself lying on a blanket on the stone floor of a half-demolished farm building, a sort of dilapidated cow-house.

As he raised his aching head he saw that milk, bread, and brandy had been left on the floor beside him; also a packet of cigarettes, some matches, and a tablet of chocolate. He drank greedily of the milk; then he took a sip of brandy and staggered to his feet. Though giddy and trembling, he found he could stand. And as he stood he noticed that he was stripped to the skin. There was not a stitch of clothing on him, nor was there a vestige of his own uniform anywhere to be seen. There was nothing but a pair of muddy yellow boots standing in the middle of the floor—boots that reminded him of those he had seen on the dying German on the hill-side. These and the grey blanket he had lain on were all that one could possibly clothe oneself in. Nothing that had been his was there. Even the brandy was not in his own flask.

Florian looked round the deserted place, the crumbling walls which bomb and shell had battered. There was a rusty, broken plough in a corner, a few tools and some odd pots and pans. After brief reflection Florian put on the boots; then he finished the bread, the milk, and the brandy. Finally, having knotted in one corner of the blanket the chocolate, the cigarettes, and the matches, he wound the rough grey covering round his body and stepped out to face the world.

It was an empty, desolate world; a dead horse lay not far off on the muddy road leading across the plain. By the sun, Florian judged it to be about seven o'clock in the morning. He seemed to recognize the locality; it might be a mile or two from the fighting ground of the preceding day. Yes. There to the left was the straight white road from Poperinghe to Ypres; he recognized the double line of trees ... where was he to go? In what direction were the Belgian lines, he wondered. He still felt weak, and his knees trembled; his mind was vacant except for a jumble of meaningless sounds. The words the dying German had repeated through the night rang in his head continually. He found himself murmuring over and over again, *"Die Flundern werden sich wundern...."*

He also had to make a strenuous mental effort to realize that he actually was wandering about the world in nothing but a pair of boots and a blanket. Everything seemed like an insensate dream. Perhaps he was still suffering from shock and dreaming all this? Perhaps he was really lying in hospital with concussion of the brain.... Who on earth could have stolen all his clothes and left him in exchange the milk, the chocolate, and the cigarettes?

There was something base and treacherous in robbing an unconscious man, he said to himself. On the other hand, there was a touch of friendliness and kindness in the chocolate and the cigarettes. The whole thing was absurd and fantastic.

"Either," reasoned Florian, stumbling along in his blanket in the direction of a distant wood, "either I have been the prey of some demented creature, or I am at this very moment light-headed myself...." *"Die Flundern werden sich wundern."* He had to make an effort not to say those crazy words aloud. He felt he would go mad if he did so. As long as he kept them shut up in his brain he was their master; but if he let them out he felt they would get the better of him, and he would go on saying them over and over and over again like the delirious German. Decidedly he was weak in his head, and must try to keep a firm hold on his brain. *"Die Flundern ... werden sich wundern."*

A few moments later he saw some mounted soldiers riding out of the wood; he saw at once that it was a German patrol. He thought of turning back and hiding in the shed again, but it was too late. They had caught sight of him, and were riding down towards him at full speed.

Well, the game was up, said Florian to himself; he would be taken. He could neither kill others nor himself with a piece of chocolate and a packet of Josetti.

So he stood stock-still, folded his arms, and awaited their arrival. (*"Die Flundern werden sich wundern...."*)

As the eight or ten men galloped up, Florian noted from afar their looks of amazement at the sight of him. They hailed him in German, and he did not reply. He stood like a statue; he said to himself that he would meet his fate with dignity. But he had not reckoned with the ludicrous effect of his attire. Two of the men dismounted, and one of them addressed him in German with a broad grin on his face; but the other—a young officer—silenced the first one abruptly, and turning a grim countenance to Florian, asked him in French why he was in that array.

"What have you done with your uniform?" he asked, scowling.

Florian scowled back at him, and gave no reply. He had made up his mind that he would not speak. (*"Die Flundern werden sich wundern."*)

The officer gave an order, and two soldiers took him by the arms and dragged his blanket from him. He stood there in his muddy boots, bare in the sunshine, his face and hands and hair caked with mud. But he was a fine and handsome figure for all that.

The officer and the men had turned their attention to the knot in the blanket. They undid it and took out the contents of the improvised pocket.

Then they looked at the figure before them and at each other. The chocolate was German; the cigarettes were German; the boots were German. What was the man?

"*Meschugge*," murmured the lieutenant in explanation, not of Florian's nationality, but of his condition of mind.

"*Meschugge! Meschugge!*" repeated the others, laughing.

The officer seemed uncertain. He turned and spoke in a low voice to the others. Florian knew they were discussing him. Would they arrest him as a cunning Belgian who had discarded his uniform, stolen the boots and the blanket, and was shamming to be insane and dumb? Or would they think him a German gone daft and send him to an infirmary? He hoped so. It would be easier to make one's escape from an infirmary than from a German prison. A German prison! Florian clenched his teeth. He saw that the officer seemed inclined to adopt this course.

"*Die Flundern werden*—" He almost said it aloud. The sound of these guttural German voices round him seemed to drag the words out of him. He felt his lips moving and he saw them watching him closely.... Suddenly the crazy words ran out of his mouth. *"Die Flundern werden sich wundern!"*

He was not prepared for the effect of those words. The soldiers burst into loud laughter; even the officer's hard face relaxed and he smiled broadly. The others repeated it with comments. "Did you hear? *'Die Flundern'*!... He has the Ueberbrettel on the brain!" And they roared with laughter and clapped him on the bare shoulders and asked him in what *Kabarett* he had left his heart and his senses.

Florian understood not a word, but he knew he was safe. At least, for the present.

Whatever the words were, they had saved him, and he made up his mind that for the time being he would use no others. A little later he added one other word to his repertoire, and that was *Meschugge*, which is Berlin dialect for mad. He himself had no faint idea of what it meant, but he heard it pronounced, evidently in regard to himself, by the Prussian Lieutenant in whose charge he was conducted back to the German lines.

"Die Flundern werden sich wundern," and *"Meschugge."* With those six words, murmured at intervals once or twice in a day, he got through the rear lines of the German army, and through a brief stay in a camp hospital, and finally into a Liège infirmary. Those who heard him knew there could be no mistake. He was no Belgian and no Frenchman. Of all words in the rich German vocabulary, of all lines of German verse or song, no foreigner in the world could ever have hit on just these. None but a true son of the Fatherland —indeed none but a pure-blooded *Berliner*—would have even known what they meant.

"Ein famoser Kerl," was this young Adonis, who had turned up from heaven knows where in a blanket and a pair of boots. *"Ein ganz famoser Kerl!"* And they clapped him on the shoulders. *"Er lebe hoch!"*

Thus it came about that the Water-corpse and Mélanie of the Café des Westens unwittingly saved the life of a gallant Belgian soldier. And as this is the only good deed they are ever likely to perform, may it stand to their credit on the Day of Judgment when they are summoned to account for their wretched and unprofitable lives.

CHAPTER XXI

On the 1st of May the Ourthe and the Aisne, each with a crisp Spring wave to its waters, came together at Bomal. "Here I am, as fresh as ever," said the frisky little Aisne.

"Oh, come off the rocks," grumbled the Ourthe, elbowing her way towards the bridge, "and don't be so gushing."

"There's a stork passing over us with a May-baby in his beak," bubbled the Aisne.

"A good thing if he dropped it. Here I am very deep," quoth the Ourthe.

The Aisne, who was not deep at all, did not understand the quibble. "How very blue you are!" she gurgled. "What is the matter? Is it going to rain?"

"If it does, mind you keep to your bed," retorted the Ourthe sarcastically.

"I won't. I am coming into yours," plashed the Aisne; and did so.

"Oh! The Meuse take you!" grumbled the Ourthe foaming and swelling.

And they went on together, quarrelling all the way to Liège, where the Meuse took them both.

The stork flew across the bridge, and stopped over Dr. Brandès's house.

"Open your eyes, little human child," said the stork. "This is where you are born."

"Rockaby, lullaby, bees in the clover...." sang Nurse Elliot, of the American Red Cross, rocking the cradle with her foot and looking dreamily out of the window. From where she sat she could catch a glimpse of the Bomal church steeple and the swaying tops of the trees in the cemetery.

"Perhaps this poor lamb would be better off if it were already asleep over there under those trees," reflected Nurse Caroline Elliot. And as if in assent, the infant in the cradle uttered a melancholy wail.

Nurse Elliot immediately began to sing Bliss Carman's May-song:

Day comes, May comes,
One who was away comes,
All the world is fair again,
Fair and kind to me.

Day comes, May comes,
One who was away comes,
Set his place at hearth and board
As it used to be.

May comes, day comes, One
who was away comes,
Higher are the hills of home,
Bluer is the sea.

The baby soon gave up all attempt to compete with the powerful American contralto, and with puckered brow and tiny clenched fist went mournfully to sleep again. He had been in the world just seven days and had not found much to rejoice over. Life seemed to consist of a good deal of noise and discomfort and bumping about. There seemed to be not much food, a great deal of singing, and a variety of aches. "I wish I were back in the land of Neverness," wept the baby, "lying in the cup of a lotus-flower in the blue morning of inexistence."

The stork, still standing on one leg on the roof resting from its journey, heard this and said: "Never mind. Cheer up. It is not for long."

"For how long is it?" asked the baby anxiously.

"Oh, less than a hundred years," said the stork, combing the feathers of its breast with its beak.

Then the baby wept even more bitterly. "Why? Why, for so short a time?" it cried.

"You bother me," said the stork; and flew away.

And the cradle rocked and the baby wept and Miss Caroline Elliot sang.

They had arrived in Bomal ten days before—Louise, Chérie and Mireille—after a nightmare journey, through Holland and Flanders. At the station in Liège, Chérie, who was very ill, aroused the compassionate attention of the American Red Cross nurses and they obtained permission to bring her in a motor ambulance to Bomal. Nurse Elliot, a tall kind woman, accompanied her, and was permitted to remain with her and assist her during the ordeal of the ensuing days.

On their arrival Louise had not come straight to the house. She had not dared to bring Mireille to her home. She feared she knew not what. Would the child recognize the place? Would the unconscious eyes perceive and recognize the surroundings that had witnessed her martyrdom? What effect might such a shock have on that stricken, sensitive soul?... Louise felt unable to face any new emotions after the fatigue and misery of the journey and the hourly anxiety in regard to Chérie.

So she accompanied Mireille to the home of their old friend, Madame Doré.

Doubtful of the welcome she would receive, fearful of the changes she might find, Louise knocked with trembling hand at the door of her old friend's house.

Madame Doré herself opened the door to her. But—was this Madame Doré? This haggard, white-haired woman, who stared at her with such startled eyes?

"Madame Doré! It is I—Louise and little Mireille! Do you not recognize us?"

"Hush! Come in." The woman drew them quickly into the passage and locked the door. Her eyes had a roving, frightened look, and every now and then a nervous spasm contracted her face.

"Oh my dear, my dear," said Louise, embracing her with tears.

Locked in Madame Doré's bedroom—for the terrorized woman had the obsession of being constantly watched and spied upon—Louise heard her friend's tragic story and recounted her own. With pitying tears Madame Doré caressed Mireille's soft hair and assured Louise that it would be a joy for her and for Jeannette to keep her with them.

"Dear little Jeannette!" exclaimed Louise. "How glad I shall be to see her again. Is she well?"

Yes. Jeannette was well.

"And Cécile—? You say she is in England?"

"Yes. She went with four or five other women from Bomal and Hamoir. She could not live here any longer; her heart was broken. She never got over the murder of her brother André"—the painful spasm distorted the careworn face again—"you knew that he was shot by the side of the poor old Curé that night in the Place de l'Église?"

Yes. Louise knew. And she pressed the hand of her old friend with compassionate tenderness. They talked of all their friends and acquaintances.

The storm had swept over them, wrecking, ruining and scattering them far and wide.

"Hush, listen!" whispered Madame Doré, suddenly grasping Louise's arm. Outside they could hear the measured tread of feet and the sound of loud voices, the loathed and dreaded German voices raised in talk and laughter.

"Our masters!" whispered Madame Doré. "They enter our houses when they choose, they come in the middle of the night and rummage through our things. They take away our money and our jewels. They read our letters, they order us about and insult us. We cannot speak or think or breathe without their knowledge and permission. They are constantly threatening us with imprisonment or with deportation. We are slaves and half-starved. Ah!" cried the unhappy woman, "why did I not have the courage to go with Cécile to England? I don't know ... I felt old, old and frightened.... And now Jeannette and I are here as in a prison, and Cécile is far away and alone."

Louise soothed her as best she could with caresses and consoling words. But Madame Doré was heart-stricken and desolate, and the fact that they had never met Cécile when they were in London caused her bitter disappointment. Perhaps some evil had befallen Cécile? Did Louise think she was safe? The English were kind, were they not?

Yes, Louise was sure Cécile was safe. And yes, the English were very kind.

Even as she spoke a rush of longing came over her; a feeling that resembled home-sickness in its tenderness and yearning. England!—ah, England! How safe, indeed, how safe and kind and cool in its girdle of grey water!...

Perhaps, mused Louise, as she hurried home alone, meeting the inquisitive glance of strangers and the insolent stare of German soldiers in the familiar village-streets, perhaps it would have been better after all if they had remained safely in England, if they had disregarded the warning of the invader and allowed him to confiscate their home. Thus at least they would have remained beyond the reach of his intrusions, his insults and his cruelty.

Meanwhile, in Dr. Brandès's house the energetic and capable Miss Elliot had not been idle. A quick survey of the ransacked abode had shown her that, although most of the valuables and all the silver and pictures had been stolen, the necessary household utensils, and even the linen, were left. Briskly and cheerfully she settled Chérie in a snow-white bed, brushed and braided her shining hair in two long plaits, gave her a cup of bread-and-milk and set resolutely to work to clear away some of the litter and confusion before Louise should arrive.

There were dirty plates and glasses, and empty bottles everywhere; there were muddy mattresses on the floor. People seemed to have slept and eaten in every room in the house. Tables, carpets and beds were strewn with cigar and cigarette-stumps; drawers and wardrobes had been emptied and their contents scattered on the floor; basins of dirty water stood on cabinets, sideboard and chairs.

Caroline Elliot brushed and emptied and cleared and cleaned, and drew in the shutters, and opened the windows, and lit the fires; and by the time she heard Louise's hurrying footsteps, was able to stand aside with a little smile of satisfaction and watch Louise's pale face light up with emotion and pleasure.

It was home, home after all!

And Louise, looking round the familiar rooms, felt a tremor of hope—the timid hope of better days to come—stir in the depths of her thankful heart.

CHAPTER XXII

The child was three weeks old and still Chérie had not seen either friend or acquaintance, nor had she dared to go out of the house. She felt too shy to show herself in the day-time, and after nightfall the inhabitants of Bomal were forbidden to leave their homes. Chérie dreaded meeting any of her acquaintances; true, there were not many left in the village, for some had taken refuge abroad and others had gone to live in the larger cities, Liège and Brussels, where, rightly or wrongly, they hoped to feel less bitterly their state of subservience and slavery.

It was a sunny afternoon towards the end of May that Nurse Elliot at last packed her neat bag and made ready to leave them.

"I cannot possibly stay a day longer," she said, caressing Chérie, who clung to her in tears. "I must go back to my post in Liège. Besides, you do not need me any more."

"Oh, I need you. I need you!" cried Chérie. "I shall be so lonely and forlorn."

"Lonely? With your child? And with your sister-in-law? Nonsense," said the nurse briskly.

"But Louise hardly speaks to me," said Chérie miserably. "She hates the child, and she hates me."

"Nonsense," said the nurse again; but she felt that there was some truth in Chérie's words.

Indeed, it was impossible not to notice the almost morbid aversion Louise felt towards the poor little intruder. Louise herself, strive as she would to hide or conquer her feeling, could not do so. Every line and feature of the tiny face, every tendril of its silky pale-gold hair, its small, pouting mouth, its strange, very light grey eyes—all, all was hateful and horrible to her. When she saw Chérie lift it up and kiss it she felt herself turn pale and sick. When she saw it at Chérie's breast, saw the small head moving, the tiny hands searching and pressing, she shuddered with horror and repugnance. Though she said to herself that this was unreasonable, that it was cruel and wrong, still the feeling was unconquerable; it seemed to spring from the innermost depths of her Belgian soul. Her hatred was as much a primitive ingenerate instinct, as was the passionate maternal love an essence of the soul of Chérie.

"She hates us, Nurse Elliot, she hates us," asseverated Chérie, pressing her clasped hands to her breast in a pitiful gesture of despair. "Sometimes if for a moment I forget how miserable I am, and I lift the little one up in my arms, and laugh at him and caress him, suddenly I feel Louise's eyes fixed upon us, cold, hostile, implacable. Yes. She hates us! And I suppose every one will hate us. Every one will turn from the child and from me in loathing and disgust. Where shall we go? Where shall we hide, I and this poor little baby of mine?" She turned a tearful glance toward the red-curtained door that hid her little one, awake and cooing in his cot. Nurse Elliot had finished packing and locking her bag, had rolled and strapped her cloak, tied on her bonnet and was ready to go to the station.

"Chérie," she said gravely, placing both her hands on the girl's frail shoulders, "whatever is in store for you, you will have to face it. And now," she added, kissing her on both cheeks, "if you love me a little, if I have really been of any help or comfort to you during these sad days, the moment has come for you to repay me."

"Oh, how—how can I ever repay you?" cried Chérie.

"By putting on your hat, taking your baby in your arms and accompanying me to the station."

"To the station! I! with—Oh, I could not, I could not!" She shrank back and a burning flush rose to her brow.

At that moment Louise entered the room dressed to go out.

"You will accompany me to the station," repeated Nurse Elliot firmly to Chérie. "You, and your sister-in-law, and the baby will all come to see me off and wish me luck."

"Don't—don't ask that," murmured Chérie.

"I do ask it," said Caroline Elliot. "And you cannot refuse. I have given you many days and many nights out of my life, and much love and tender anxiety. And this is the only thanks I shall ever ask." She stepped close to Chérie and placed her arms around her. "Can you not see, my dear, that sooner or later you will be forced to meet the ordeal you dread? You cannot imprison yourself and the child for ever between these four walls. Then take your courage and face the world today; now, while I am still with you."

Chérie stood pale and hesitant; then she turned to Louise. "Would you—would you go with me?"

There was so much humility and misery in her voice that Louise was touched.

"Of course I will," she said; "go quickly and get ready."

Chérie ran to her room. She put on the modest black frock she had worn on the journey from England, but she dressed the baby in all his prettiest clothes—the white cape she had embroidered for him, and the lace cap with blue ribbons and the smartest of his blue silk socks. She lifted him in her arms and stepped before the mirror. After all it was a very sweet baby, was it not? People might hate him when they heard of him, but when they saw him....

Trembling, blushing and smiling she appeared at the gate where Miss Elliot and Louise stood waiting for her. She stepped timidly out of doors between them, and very young and very pathetic did she look with her flushed cheeks and shining, diffident eyes. Whom would they meet? Would they see any one they knew?

Yes. They met Mademoiselle Vcraender, the school-mistress, who looked at them, started, looked again and then, blushing crimson, crossed to the other side of the road. They met Madame Linkaerts and her daughter Marie. The girl recognized them with a cry of delight, but her mother took her brusquely by the arm and turned her brusquely down a side-street. They met four German soldiers strolling along who stared first at the American nurse, then at Louise, then at Chérie with the baby in her arms.

One of them made a remark and the others laughed. They stood still to let the three women pass, and the one who had spoken waved his fingers at Chérie. *"Ein Vaterlandskindlein?—nicht wahr?"* And he threw a kiss to the child.

Three or four street-urchins who had been following the soldiers, imitating their strutting gait and sticking their tongues out at them, noticed the greeting and interpreted it with the sharpness which characterizes the gutter-snipe all the world over. They also began to throw kisses to Chérie and to the baby, shouting, *"Petit boche? Quoi?"* A lame elderly man passed and taking in the situation at a glance, ran after the boys with his stick. Others passed, and stopped. Many of them recognized the women, and some looked pityingly, others contemptuously at the flushed and miserable Chérie. But no one came to speak to her, no one greeted her, no one smiled at the child in its embroidered cape and its cap with the blue ribbons. A few idlers making rude remarks, followed them to the station.

Nurse Elliot left them. It was a sad leave-taking. Then they returned home in silence, going far out of their way to choose the least frequented streets.

As they came down the shady lane behind their house Louise glanced at Chérie, and her heart melted with pity. What a child she looked for her nineteen years! And how sad and frightened and ashamed? What could Louise do to help her? What consolation could she offer? What hope could she hold out?

None. None. Except that the child should die. And why should it die? Was it not the child of puissant youth, of brutal vitality? Did it not drink its sustenance from the purest source of life? Why should it die?

No; the child would live; live to do harm and hurt; to bring sorrow and shame on them all. Live to keep the flame of hatred alight in their hearts, to remind them for ever of the foul wrong they had suffered....

Chérie had felt Louise's eyes upon her and turned to her quickly. Had not her sensitive soul perceived a passing breath of pity and of tenderness? Surely Louise would turn to her now with a word of consolation and compassion? Perhaps the sight of her helpless infant had touched Louise's heart at last....

No, no. Again she caught that look of resentment, that terrible look of anger and shame in Louise's eyes; and bending her head lower over her child she hurried into the house.

CHAPTER XXIII

The house seemed very empty without Nurse Elliot. Chérie seldom spoke, for she had nothing to speak about but her baby, and she knew that to such talk Louise would neither wish to listen nor reply.

Other mothers, reflected Chérie bitterly, could speak all day about their children, and she, also, would have loved to tell of all the wonderful things she discovered in her baby day by day. For instance, he always laughed in his dreams, which meant that the angels still spoke to him; and the soles of his tiny feet were quite pink; and he had a dimple in his left cheek, and a quantity of silky golden hair on the nape of his neck—all things that Louise had never noticed, and Chérie did not dare to speak about them. There was silence, pitiless silence, round that woeful cradle.

In order that the child should not disturb Louise, Chérie had given up her own bedroom and chosen for the nursery the spare room on the floor below—the room with the red curtains—which, strangely enough, seemed for her to hold no memories. One afternoon as she sat there nursing her child, Louise, who hardly ever crossed that threshold, opened the door and came in.

Chérie looked up with a welcoming smile of surprise and joy. But Louise turned her eyes away from her and from the slumbering babe.

"I have come to tell you," she said, "that Mireille is coming home. I am going to fetch her this evening."

Chérie drew a quick breath of alarm. "Mireille!... Mireille is coming here?" she exclaimed.

"Surely you did not expect the poor child to stay away for ever?" said Louise, her eyes filling with tears. "I have missed her very much," she added bitterly.

"Of course ... of course," stammered Chérie, "I am sorry!... But what is ... what is to become of me? I mean, what shall we do, the baby and I?"

"What *can* you do?" said Louise bitterly.

Chérie bent over her child. "I wish we could hide" ... she said in a low voice, "hide ourselves away where nobody would ever see us."

Louise made no reply. She sat down, turning away from Chérie, and tried not to feel pitiless. "Harden not your hearts ... harden not your hearts ..." she repeated to herself, striving to stifle the sense of implacable rancour, of bitter hatred which hurt her own heart, but which she could not overcome.

"Mireille will come here!" Chérie repeated under her breath. "She will see the child! What will she say? What will she say?"

Louise raised her sombre eyes and drew a deep breath of pain.

"Alas! She will say nothing, poor little Mireille! She will say nothing." And the bitter thought of Mireille's affliction overwhelmed her mother's soul.

No; whatever happened Mireille, once such a joyous, laughter-loving sprite, would say nothing. She would see Chérie with a baby in her arms, and would say nothing. She would see her mother kneeling at her feet beseeching for a word, and would say nothing. Her father might return, and she would be silent; or he might die—and she would not open her lips. This other child, this child of shame and sorrow, would grow up and learn to speak, would smile and laugh and call Chérie by the sweet-sounding name by which Louise would never be called again, but Mireille would be for ever silent.

Chérie had risen with her baby in her arms. Shy and trembling she went to Louise and knelt at her feet.

"Louise! Louise! Can you not love us and forgive us? What have we done? What has this poor little creature done to you that you should hate it so? Louise, it is not for me that I implore your pity and your love; I can live without them if I must; I can live despised and hated because I know and understand. But for him I implore you! For this poor innocent who has done no harm, who has come into life branded and ill-fated, and does not know that he may not be loved as other children are—one word of tenderness, Louise, one word of blessing!"

She caught at Louise's dress with her trembling hand. "Louise, lay your hand on his forehead and say 'God bless you.' Just those three little words that every one says to the poorest and the most wretched. Just say that shortest of all prayers for him!"

There was silence.

"Louise!" sobbed Chérie, "if you were to say that, I think it would help him and me to live through all the days of misery to come. It is so sad, Louise, that no one, no one should ever have invoked a benediction upon so poor and helpless a child."

Louise's eyes filled with tears. She looked down at the tiny face and the strange light eyes blinked up at her. They were cruel eyes. They were the eyes she had seen glaring at her across the room, mocking and taunting her, at that supreme instant when her prayers and little Mireille's had at last succeeded in touching their oppressor's heart. Those eyes, those light grey eyes in the ruthless face had lit upon her, hard as flint, cruel as a blade of steel: "The seal of Germany must be set upon the enemy's country——"

Those eyes had condemned her to her doom.

"I cannot, I cannot," she said, and turned away.

CHAPTER XXIV

Dusk was falling and a thin grey mist crept up from the two rivers as Louise, with a black scarf over her head, hurried out of the house to fetch Mireille. She was about to turn down the narrow rue de la Pompe which led straight to the house of Madame Doré without passing the Place de l'Église, where at this hour all the German soldiers were assembled, when she noticed the hunched-up figure of a Flemish peasant coming slowly along the small alley. He seemed to be mumbling to himself, and looked such a strange figure with his slouch hat and limping gait that in order to avoid him she turned back and went through the Square where the soldiers lounged and smoked. They paid no heed to her and she hurried on.

In her heart a wild new hope had sprung. She was going to bring Mireille home. For the first time since that terrible morning of their flight, Mireille would find herself once more in the surroundings that had witnessed her martyrdom.

What if the shock of entering that house again, of being face to face with all that must remind her of the struggle in which her agonized child-spirit had been wrecked, what if that shock—Louise scarcely dared to formulate the wild hope even in her own mind—were to heal her? Such things had happened. Louise had heard and read of them; of people who were mad and had suddenly been restored to reason, of people who were dumb and had recovered their speech through some sudden powerful emotion.

With beating heart Louise went faster through the silent streets.

The man she had seen in the rue de la Pompe had limped on; then turning to the right he had found himself in front of Dr. Brandès's house.

He stopped and looked up at the windows. They were open, wide open to the cool evening air, and at the sight, joy rushed into his heart. The house was certainly inhabited. By whom? By whom?... Had they reached Bomal after all? He had heard from Claude that they had left England to return to their home. Had they arrived safely? Were they here?

The hope of seeing them again had inspired him to attempt and achieve his daring flight from the Infirmary at Liège, and his temerarious almost incredible journey across miles of closely-guarded country. The vision of Chérie had been before him when at dead of night, with bleeding hands, he had worked for hours to loosen the meshes of wire nets and entanglements that surrounded the hospital grounds, where—half patient, half prisoner—he had been held under strict surveillance for nearly a month. It was Chérie's white hand that had beckoned to him and upheld him through the long hungry days and the dreary nights, when he was hiding in woods, crouching in ditches, plunging into rivers, scrambling over walls and rocks until he had reached the valley of the Aisne—passing indeed, quite near to Roche-à-Frêne where, he remembered, she had gone for an excursion on her last birthday…. It was the thought of Chérie that had inspired and guided him through untold risks and dangers. And now, perhaps, she was here, here in this house before him, within reach of his voice, within sight of his eyes, just beyond those joyous open windows….

He remembered how on her birthday-night less than a year ago he had clattered up on horseback through the quiet streets and had seen these windows wide open as they were now.—Ah, what destruction had swept over the world since then!

He remembered the sound of those laughing, girlish voices:

Sur le pont
D'Avignon
On y danse
On y danse….

He glanced quickly round, then he raised his head and softly whistled the well-known tune.

Chérie had remained alone. She had heard Louise leave the house, closing the outer door, and the sound of her quick footsteps had reached her for a while from the street. Then silence had fallen.

Louise was going to fetch Mireille. Soon they would come back together, and Chérie must decide what she would do. How should she face Mireille? No; she must hide, hide with her child, so that Mireille should not see him. For what would Mireille say when she saw the child? True, as Louise said, she would say nothing—nothing that ears could hear. But what would her soul say? How could any one know what Mireille saw and what she did not see? Who could tell but what she might not see and remember and hate, even as Louise hated? And that silent hatred would be still more terrible to bear. Yes; Mireille would surely know when she saw those very light eyes that opened so widely in the tiny face; she would remember the man who had tortured her, who had bound her to the iron banisters with her face turned to the bedroom door—this very door, close by, draped with the red curtains—Yes. The memory and the horror of it all would come back to her wandering spirit every time she saw those strange light eyes, now half-closed as the small head nestled sleepily at its mother's breast.

Chérie bent over her child and kissed the fair hair and the drowsy eyes and the sweet half-open mouth. What if every one hated him? She loved him. She loved him with the love of all mothers and with the greater love of her sorrow and despair and shame.

"Child of mine," she whispered, "why did they not let us both drift away into eternity on that May morning when you had not yet crossed the threshold of life, and I was so near to the open doors of death? We could have floated peacefully away together, you and I, out of all this trouble and sorrow. How simple and restful it would have been."

But her baby slept and it was dusk and bed-time; so she rose and carried him to his cradle in the adjoining room, pushing the red curtains aside with her elbow as she entered.

While she did so she found herself vaguely thinking of her birthday-night, of the dance with Jeannette, Cri-cri, Cécile. Like a bright disconnected thread that memory seemed to run through her dark thoughts. What had brought it into her mind? Why was she suddenly living over again that brief happy hour before the storm broke over her and wrecked her life?

The gay senseless words of the old dance kept ringing in her mind.

> Sur le pont
> D'Avignon
> On y danse
> Tout en rond....

A thrill passed through her as she realized that some passer-by was whistling it in the street. Tears gathered in her eyes at the memories which that puerile tune evoked.

> Sur le pont
> D'Avignon
> On y danse
> On y danse,
> Sur le pont
> D'Avignon
> On y danse
> Tout en rond.

Soft and clear the whistling still persisted. Chérie placed the baby in its cradle, stooped over him and kissed him. Then she went to the window and stood on tiptoe to look out—for the window was high and round, like a ship's porthole.

The whistling stopped. Somebody standing in the shadow of the wall stepped forward.

And Chérie's heart stood still.

CHAPTER XXV

She staggered back from the window and looked wildly round her. It was Florian. It was Florian! What should she do? The child—where could she hide the child?

The low whistle outside was repeated, there was a note of haste, of urgency in it. She must let him in. How had he got here? Surely he was in danger, there in the open street....

Chérie looked at herself, looked down at her loose white gown still unfastened at neck and breast—the child's warm white resting-place. Louise's black shawl lay across a chair. She took it and flung it hastily round her shoulders; holding it tightly about her as she ran down the stairs and opened the door.

Florian stepped quickly into the passage, closing the door behind him. He looked strange in his oil-skin coat and slouch hat. The glimpse Chérie caught of his face as he entered showed it hard and thin and dark. Now in the shadowy passage she could not distinguish his features.

He caught her hand and pressed it tightly in his own. "Chérie!... Chérie!" His voice was hoarse with emotion. "Who is here with you?" he whispered.

"Nobody," she replied.

"What? Are you alone in the house?"

"Yes," faltered Chérie, withdrawing her hand from his. "I mean...." and she stopped.

"Surely," he whispered anxiously, "you are not living here alone? Where are the others? Where is Louise?"

"She is here—she has gone out. She will soon come back."

Florian drew a sigh of relief. "Let us go upstairs," he said; and stretched out his hand to take hers again. "What a cold little hand! And how you tremble!" He bent down and looked closely into her face. "Did I frighten you?"

"Yes," said Chérie.

"You look like a ghost." Suddenly a different note came into his voice, a note of anxiety and alarm. "What is the matter, have you been ill?"

"Yes," breathed Chérie.

He asked nothing more but put his arm round her, helping and hurrying her up the two flights of stone stairs. He threw open the sitting-room door and looked round the familiar place. "The Saints be praised," he murmured, and drew her into the room.

He flung down his torn felt hat and threw off the long oil-skin coat. Under it he was dressed in a dark linen suit, such as she had seen some of the wounded Germans wear. He drew her to the window seat; the soft May twilight fell on her pale face and glittering hair.

"Tell me, Chérie, tell me all the news; quickly. I cannot stay long," he added, "it would be dangerous for you and for me. I have escaped from the Infirmary at Liège; they will be hunting all over the place for me—and for the ploughman's clothes," he added with a smile that for a moment made him look like the Florian of old.

"The Infirmary? Have you been wounded?"

"No. I have been blown up. The Germans found me; they think me a Boche, and *meschugge*—that is Berlinese for crazy. They have kept me with ice-bags on my head for three weeks," he laughed again. "Perhaps I was really off my head at first—but tell me, tell me about you. How are you? How is Louise?"

"She is well."

"Is the little girl here too?"

"Mireille?" There was a pause. "Yes, Mireille is here."

Something in her voice startled him. "What is wrong? Has anything happened?"

She was silent. His steel-blue eyes tried to pierce through the pallor of her face, through the black-fringed, drooping eyelids, to read in her soul. He suddenly felt that this shrinking figure in its white gown and black shawl was aloof from him and draped in mystery. "What is it?" he repeated. "What is wrong? Where has Louise gone to?" and he looked round the familiar room with a sense of misgiving.

"She has gone ... to ... to fetch Mireille...." Chérie stammered. Then she suddenly raised her wild blue eyes to his. "Mireille is not as she used to be."

"What do you mean?" Florian suddenly felt sick and dizzy.

"She does not know any one. And she does not speak."

"Not speak?" echoed Florian, and the sense of sickness and dread increased. "What has happened to her?"

"She was frightened...." Chérie's voice was toneless and he had to bend close to her to catch her words. "She was frightened ... that night you left ... my birthday night." ... There was a silence. She could say no more. And suddenly Florian was silent too.

His silence seemed to fall on her heart like a heavy stone. At last she raised her eyes to his face.

"Speak," he said, "speak quickly."

"That night ... they ... they came here...."

"I know. I know *they* came through Bomal." The cold sweat stood on his brow. "Did they—come to this house?"

"Yes," said Chérie.

Again there was silence—heavy and portentous.

Then he rose to his feet and stood a little away from her.

"They were in this house," he repeated. His lips and throat were arid; he had the sensation that his voice came from afar off. "What—what happened to Mireille? Did they hurt her?"

"No. She was afraid ... she screamed ... and they tied her to that railing. There"—she pointed with her trembling hand to the wrought-iron banister.

And again Florian's silence fell upon her heart like a rock and lay there, heavily, crushing the life out of her.

After a long while he moved. He stepped back still further from her, and his lips stirred once or twice before the words came.

"And you? Did they—harm you?"

Silence.

He waited a long time, then he repeated the question; and again he felt as if his voice came from miles away.

Chérie suddenly dropped her face in her hands. He was answered. He sprang forward and seized her wrists, dragging them away from her face. "It is not true," he cried; "swear that it is not true!" And even as he spoke he felt and hated the soft limp wrists, the feminine weakness, all the delicate yielding frailty of her. He would have liked to feel her of steel and adamant, that he might break and shatter her, that he might crush and destroy.

Now she was at his feet, sobbing and crying; and he had clenched his fists so tightly in order not to strike her that his nails dug deep into his palms. He looked down at her shimmering hair, at the white nape of her neck, at her fragile, heaving shoulders. The enemy had had her. The enemy had had her and held her. She whom he had deemed too sacred for his touch, she whom he had never dared to kiss on cheek or hair or lips had quenched the brutish desire of the invader!… The foul, blood-drunken soldiers had had their will of her—and there she lay sullied, ruined, and defiled.

With a cry like the cry of a wounded animal he raised his clenched fists to heaven, and the blood from his lacerated palms ran down his wrists, and the tears, the hot searing tears that corrode a man's soul, rolled down his gaunt, agonized face.

There she lay, the broken, helpless creature, there she lay—the symbol of his country, his wrecked and ruined country!

Lost, lost both of them—broken, outraged and defiled.

Not all his blood, not all his prayers, could ever undo the wrong that had been done to them, could ever raise them in their pristine glory and purity—the sullied soul of the woman, the outraged heart of his land.

In the grey gloaming that fell around them, veiling with its shadows the shame of her face, she told him what was still left to tell.

He said never a word. He sat with bowed head, his eyes hidden in his hands. He felt as if he were dead in a dead world. All the flames of his anger and despair were spent. His soul was turned to ashes. Nothing was left. Nothing was left to live for, to fight for, to pray for.

For a long time he seemed to hear none of the stricken woman's words, as she knelt sobbing at his feet. Then one word, constantly recurring, beat on his brain like a hammer on red-hot iron.

"The child … the child"—every other word that fell from her lips seemed to be "the child."

"If only I could die," she was crying, "I should love to die were it not for the child. It is such a forlorn and desolate little child. Nobody ever looks at it, nobody ever smiles at it or wishes it well…. Not even Louise, who is so kind…. No, she is cruel, she is like a fury when she looks at the child. Oh, God! what will our life be in the midst of so much scorn and hatred? Not that I care about myself; but what will become of the little child? Perhaps I should have done as Louise did…. I should have torn it from me before it came to life."

A deep shudder ran through Florian.

"But I seemed to hear a voice in my soul—the very voice of God, calling aloud to me: '*Thou shall not kill.*'"

Florian rose to his feet and looked down at the bowed figure. This was Chérie, the laughing, dimpling, blushing Chérie—his betrothed!… He bent over her and laid his hand on her shoulder, but she paid no heed.

"Ah, if only we could slip out of life together, the child and I! But how? How? When he looks up at me and touches my face with his tiny hands, how can I hurt him?" Her tear-flooded eyes looked up at Florian without seeing him. "Should I strangle the little tender throat with my hands? Or stifle the soft breath of his mouth?... Why should he not live like other children, and laugh and play and be happy like every other child? What has he done, poor innocent, that he should be accursed, among children, an outcast, hated and despised?"

"Chérie!" he said, but she did not hear or heed him. Nor did she heed the braggart peal of trumpet and clarionet passing under the windows with the din of the "Wacht am Rhein." She heard nothing, she cared for nothing but her own and the enemy's child.

The soldier's blood rose within him.

"And is this all you have to say to me when I come to you out of the very jaws of death? Is this all you can think of when our land is wrung and wracked by the enemy, torn to pieces by the foul fiends that have violated her and you? A thousand curses on them and on——"

"No—no—no!" she screamed, springing to her feet and covering his mouth with her hands. "No—no—not on him, not on him!"

"In the name of Belgium," roared the maddened Florian, "in the name of our outraged women, our perishing children, our murdered men, I curse the child you have borne! In the name of our broken hearts, in the name of our burned and ravaged homesteads—Louvain, Lierre, Berlaer, Mortsel, Waehlen, Weerde, Hofstade, Herselt, Diest——" The names fell from his lips, fanning his heart to fury; but the woman closed her ears with her hands so as not to hear the tragic enumeration of those sacred and familiar names—Belgium's rosary of martyrdom and fire.

She held her hands over her ears and wept: "May God not hear you!... May God not hear you!"

But he raised his voice and continued the appalling litany: "Malines, Fleron, Wavre, Notre Dame, Rosbeck, Muysen——" Suddenly he stopped. A sound had struck his ear—what was it?

It was a cry—the short, shrill cry of an infant.

The man stood still as if turned to stone; his blood-shot eyes, starting from their sockets, stared at the red-draped door from which the sound had come.

Chérie was at his feet, sobbing and wailing, her arms flung round his knees.

"Have pity, have pity!" she sobbed, shaking with terror of him, blind with the fear of his violence. "Do no harm, do no harm! Kill me, trample upon me, but do no harm to the child."

And still Florian stood motionless, as if turned to stone. He heard none of the wild words that fell from the terrified woman's lips; he heard nothing but that querulous cry, the cry of the newly-born. The world seemed to ring with it. Above the wailing voice of the woman, above the din of soldiery, the clash of arms, the roar of warfare, rose that shrill cry of life, the cry of humanity. And that cry pierced his heart like a sword. In it was all the helplessness and misery of the world. It seemed to tell him of the uselessness and hopelessness and sadness of all things.

Anger, grief and despair, the passion of vengeance and the desire to kill, all dropped out of his soul and left it silent and empty. The terrified woman before him saw those fierce eyes soften, saw the stern lips tremble.

He bent forward and raised her to her feet. "Poor Chérie!" he said. "Poor little Chérie!" He took her pale, disfigured face between his two hands and looked into her eyes. "Say good-bye to me. Say good-bye. And may the Saints protect you."

"Where are you going? What will you do?" she sobbed as she saw him turning away from her, making ready to go out into the darkness—out of her life for ever.

"There is much for me to do," he said and his eyes wandered to the window whence the sound of the German bugles could still be heard.

And as she looked at him she saw that Florian, the comrade and lover of her youth, had vanished—only the soldier stood before her, the soldier aloof from her, detached from her, the soldier alone with his stern great task to do.

But in her the woman, the eternal, helpless woman, was born again, and she clung to him and wept, for passion and love returned to her soul and overwhelmed her.

"You will leave me! You will leave me! Florian, oh, my love! What will become of me? What shall I do? What shall I do?"

As if in answer, the feeble cry of the infant rose again.

The man said not a word. He raised his hand and pointed silently to the red-draped door. Then he turned from her and went out into the night.

Chérie stood still, gazing at the empty doorway through which he had passed.

Then as the child still wept, she went to him.

Humbly she went, and took her woman's place beside the cradle.

CHAPTER XXVI

The bugle bidding the inhabitants of Bomal to enter their homes and lock their doors blew shrilly as Louise hurried through the darkening, deserted streets, holding Mireille's chilly hand in hers. She spoke in soft, hurried tones, as if the child could hear her, as if she could understand. "You shall see, Mireille, you shall see when you enter your home—you will recognize it and remember. When I open the door and you step suddenly into the familiar place, I shall see the light break in your eyes like a sudden dawn. You will turn to me and you will smile—or weep! I do not know which will give me the greater joy—your tears or your smile. Then you will open your sweet lips —and speak...."

"What will your first words be, Mireille? Will you say, 'Mother'? Will you greet me as one who returns from a long journey, as one who wakens from a long dream?... Or, even though your voice be given back to you, will you be silent awhile, able yet not daring to speak?... Or will the first sound from your lips be a cry of terror when you remember what you saw that night?... Mireille, Mireille, whatever it be, I know that this evening I shall hear your voice. It is as if God had told me so."

They went more quickly through the sombre streets.

Far away over the hills of the Ardennes the great May moon arose. As soon as Louise caught sight of the house she saw that the gate to the courtyard was open. Could any one have entered during her absence? She glanced up at the windows. They were open, but dark. The sense of panic that was never far from her heart since their return to Belgium clutched at her like a cold hand. Could anything have happened? Why had Chérie not lit the lights? Who had left the gate unclosed?

Then the thought of Mireille, the hope, the wild prescience of her recovery which had suddenly grown into a delirious certainty flamed up in her heart again, and all else was forgotten. She and Mireille were alone in the world.

She and Mireille were alone.

She kept her eyes fixed on the small vacant face as she led her past the gate— that gate through which the child's dancing feet had twinkled throughout the care-free seasons of her infancy.

But not a quiver rippled over the childish countenance, not a gleam of light flickered in the dreamy eyes, and with a low sob Louise grasped the small passive hand more tightly and drew her across the courtyard to the hall-door.

That door also was ajar, as if some one had hurriedly left it so, regardless of the invader's orders that at sunset all doors should be locked. One moment Louise thought of calling to Chérie to make sure that she was in the house; but again the need to be alone, face to face with Mireille's awakening soul, restrained her. She drew Mireille into the hall and turned on the light.

"Mireille ... Mireille...." she whispered breathlessly. "Look, darling ... don't you remember? Don't you remember?"

The girl's pale eyes roved from the tapestried archway to the panelled doors, from the ornamental panoply to the Van de Welde winter landscapes hanging on the wall before her. No ray of recognition lit the unmoved face, which was fair and still as a closed flower. With beating heart Louise placed her arm around the girl's narrow shoulders and guided her light, uncertain footsteps up the stairs. The door to the sitting-room was open; Louise stretched out her hand, and the brilliancy of the electric light lit up the room.

With a gasp Louise felt Mireille falter on the threshold ... she stood breathless and watched her. Surely, surely she must recognize this scene: there to the right, the large Flemish fireplace; there beyond it the old-fashioned oak settee; and there the shallow flight of stairs, with the wrought-iron banisters running right down into the room, facing the door with the red-tapestried curtains.... Surely, with this scene of her martyrdom brought suddenly before her, the veil of unconsciousness would be rent from her soul. Louise felt it. Louise knew it. Already she could almost hear the cry with which her child would turn to her and fall into her arms....

Nothing. Nothing happened.

For an instant a vague expression, a pale light as of dread, had flickered over the tranquil countenance. She had faltered, and stood still, with her eyes fixed on the red drapery of the closed door. Then the pale flicker of emotion had faded from her face as if blown out by a gust of wind.

Nothing more. With limp, pendant hands and vacant eyes she stood before Louise in her usual drooping posture—pale, ethereal and unreal, like a little weary seraph walking in its dreams.

The flaming torch of hope in the mother's heart was dashed to the ground.

And all was dark.

CHAPTER XXVII

Chérie, kneeling beside her child's cradle, had heard them enter the adjoining room. She rose slowly. She must go and meet them; she must greet Mireille and tell Louise that Florian had come; had come ... and gone!

The profound silence in the adjoining room struck her. She wondered, as she hesitated at the door, why Louise did not speak. For did she not always talk to Mireille in that low, tender voice of hers, as if the child could understand? Now there was not a sound. It was if the room were empty.

Suddenly she understood. Louise was waiting, hoping that the miracle might be accomplished—that Mireille might speak. Then Chérie also stood motionless with clasped hands, and waited, waited for a sound, a word, a cry.

But the silence remained unbroken.

At last she heard the sound of Louise's weeping; and, soon after, their soft, retreating footsteps on the carpeted stairs. Then utter silence.

And Chérie still stood at the closed door, leaning her forehead against its panels.

They had gone. Louise was taking Mireille to bed. She had not called Chérie. She had not said good-night, nor asked her to come and see Mireille. No. Chérie was not needed. Louise, even in her great sorrow, did not think of coming to Chérie. She had gone with Mireille to her room, and she would stay there and weep all alone, and sleep at last, never knowing that Florian had been, never knowing that he had gone away for ever, never knowing that Chérie's heart was broken!... With a rush of passionate grief Chérie drew back from the door and fell on her knees beside the cradle.

And there the great May moon, rising like a golden disc over the hills of the Ardennes, found her and shone down through the round window, upon her and her sleeping babe.

⸻

Louise, lying awake in the dark, heard the church clock strike eleven. She lay quite still in the silent room, listening to Mireille's soft breathing. Then she thought of Claude, and prayed for his safety; but not for his return.

At last, exhausted, she slept.

But Mireille, though her soft breathing never varied, was not asleep. She lay motionless in the dark, with her eyes wide open. She was listening to something that had awakened within her—Memory!...

The church clock struck half-past eleven. Louise still slept, with the occasional catch in her breath of those who have cried themselves to sleep.

Mireille sat up. The room was quite dark, the shutters closed and the curtains drawn. But Mireille slipped from her bed, a slim, white-robed spectre, and her bare feet crossed the room without a sound. She found the door and opened it noiselessly; she crossed the landing, and her small feet trod the carpeted staircase as lightly and silently as the falling petals of a flower.

Where was she going to? What drew her through the dark and silent house?

Terror—and the memory of a red-draped door. Nothing else did her haunted eyes perceive, nothing else did her stricken soul realize, but that red curtain draped over a door. She remembered it with a vague, horrible sense of fear. She must see it again.... Had she not once stood before that draped door for hours and years and eternities?... Yes. She must see it again. And if that door were to open—she must die!...

She went on, drawn by her terror as by an unseen force, until she reached the last shallow flight of stairs—three steps skirted by a wrought-iron banister—and there she stopped suddenly, as if fettered to the spot. For though the room was plunged in darkness she knew that there, opposite her, was the door with the red curtain....

And thus she stood, in the self-same attitude of her past martyrdom, feeling that she was pinioned there, feeling that she must stand for ever with her eyes fixed in the darkness on that part of the room where she knew was the door— the door with the red curtain....

Chérie heard the clock strike eleven; then the quarter; then the half-hour. And still she lay on the floor with her face hidden in her arms.

For her all was at an end. Her resolve was taken. Her mind was clear. Now she had seen Florian there was nothing left to wait for. What good would she or the child ever do in the world? Nobody wanted them. Nobody ever wanted to see them or speak to them. They were outcasts. Not even Louise could look without loathing at the hapless little child. Not even Louise could invoke a benediction upon him. He was ill-omened, hated and accursed.

Chérie rose to her feet and went to the window—the old-fashioned circular window like a ship's porthole—and opened it wide.

The level rays of the moon poured in, flooding the room with light.

"Good-night, moon," said Chérie. "Good-night, sky. Good-night, world." Then she turned away and went to the cradle. She bent over it, and lifted her sleeping infant in her arms. How warm he was! How warm and soft and tender!... He must not catch cold.... Instinctively Chérie caught up her wide blue silk scarf and wrapped it round herself and the child. They were going out into the night air, out into the chilly moonlight; they were going to cross the bridge over the Ourthe, and then go up the lower bank of the river, up through the dank grasses, past the old mill.... There, where the bank shelved down so steeply she would run into the water.

She knew what it would feel like. Last year, had she not run into the rippling waves at Westende every morning? She remembered it well.

Yes; she would feel the cool chill embrace of the water rising from her feet to her knees ... to her waist ... to her breast ... to her throat.... Then she would clasp her arms tightly round her child, putting her lips close to his so as not to hear him cry, and her last breath would be exhaled on the sweet warmth of that little mouth, the dear little open mouth that seemed always to be asking for the balm of milk and kisses.

She raised her eyes once more to the open window. "Good-bye," she said again to the sky, to the world, and to life. Then she resolutely turned away from the shining circle of light.

She drew the long blue scarf over her own head and shoulders, crossing it over her arms and wrapping the infant in its azure folds as she held him to her breast. Then she opened the door.

The red curtain fell in a straight line before her, and she pushed it softly aside; it slid smoothly back on its rings.

Clasping her infant in the shimmering folds of blue, she took a step forward—then stopped and stood transfixed in the doorway.

Some one was there! Some one was standing silent, there in the dark.

Who was it?

Mireille!

––––––––––––––––

Mireille had stood motionless, almost cataleptic, with her fear-maddened eyes fixed upon the dark spot which was the door. Now—now it was opening! it was opening! A white light had streamed suddenly under the curtain.

Yes. The door was opening…. Now Mireille would die! She knew it! What she was going to see would kill her, as it had killed her soul before.

Gasping, with open mouth, with clenched hands, she saw the gap of light widen beneath the moving curtain…. Now … now…. The curtain had slid back. There was a dazzling square of light….

And in that light stood a Vision.

Bathed in the rays of the moon, swathed in shimmering azure stood a Mother with her Child. Behind her head glowed a luminous silver circle.

Ah! Well did Mireille know her! Well did Mireille remember her. All fear was gone, all darkness swept away in the rapture of that dazzling presence.

Mireille stretched out her clasped hands towards that effulgent vision. What were the words of greeting she must say? She knew them well … they were rising in her throat…. What were they? What were they?

She wrung her clasped hands, with a spasm in her throat, but the words would not come. She knew them. They seemed to burst open like flowers of light in her brain, to peal like the notes of an organ in her soul, yet her lips were locked and could not frame them.

The vision moved, seemed to waver and tremble…. Ah! Would she fade away and vanish and be lost? Would Mireille fall back again into eternal silence and darkness?

Something seemed to break in Mireille's throat. A cry—a cry, thrilling and articulate—escaped her. The sealed fountain of her voice was opened and the words of the immortal salutation gushed from her lips:

"*Ave Maria!…*"

Did not the shimmering figure smile and move towards her with extended hand?… Fainting with ecstasy, Mireille sank at her feet.

Louise had started from her sleep at the sound of a cry…. Whose voice had uttered it?

Though the room was dark, she felt that it was empty; she knew that Mireille was not there. Yes, the door was open, showing a pale glimmer of light.

Swift as an arrow Louise sped down the stairs, then—on the landing of the last flight—she stopped, dazzled and spell-bound by what she saw before her.

There in the moonlight stood the eternal vision of Maternity; and before it knelt Mireille.

And Mireille was speaking.

"Benedicta tu...."

Clear, frail and silvern the words fell from Mireille's lips.

"Benedicta tu!"

The blessing that Louise and all others had withheld, now fell like a solemn prophecy from the innocent's lips, rang like a divine decree in that pure voice that had been hushed so long.

Mireille was healed! Healed through Chérie and her child of sorrow and shame.

A wave of exalted emotion overwhelmed Louise, and she sank on her knees beside Mireille, repeating the hallowed benediction.

With flowing tears Chérie, clasping her baby in her arms, wavered and trembled like a holy picture seen in moonlit waters....

And so farewell—farewell to Mireille, Chérie, Louise.

They are still in their Belgian village awaiting the dawn of their deliverance.

Around them the fury of War still rages, and the end of their sorrow is not yet.

But upon them has descended the Peace of God which passeth all understanding.

THE END